THE OYSTER
Volume 5

The Oyster, along with its notable predecessor *The Pearl*, was one of the leading late Victorian underground magazines.

It continued to thrive until 1896. Along with *The Pearl* and other similar magazines, these underground journals provided a platform of resistance to the suffocating, guilt-ridden climate in which they appeared. Copies of these have fortunately survived to delight and amuse us as well as to provide an unusual and unconventional insight into the manners and mores of a vanished world, the reverse side of the coin of iron-clad respectability which appeared to characterise British society some hundred years ago.

THE OYSTER V

ANONYMOUS

Carroll & Graf Publishers, Inc.
New York

Copyright © 1990 by Glenthorne Historical Research Associates

First Carroll & Graf edition 1991

Carroll & Graf Publishers, Inc.
260 Fifth Avenue
New York, NY 10001

ISBN: 0-88184-711-9

Manufactured in the United States of America

INTRODUCTION

This salacious, entertaining selection of material from *The Oyster* well illustrates the decadent, *fin de siecle* image we have of upper class society in the late Victorian era. In spite of the stifling morality of the times there were days (and nights!) of endless sauciness, a long round of gaiety for the privileged few. These were years of high jinks and low necklines and at the centre of it all was HRH the Prince of Wales.

As Godfrey Smith has commented: 'What made the Nineties naughty was a small coterie of rich, idle and sexy men and women whose life revolved around Albert Edward, Prince of Wales . . . his entourage widened over the years to admit some cosmopolitan and raffish figures: adventurers, bounders, philanderers, mistresses, courtesans and actresses.'

Yet hand in hand with the fun-loving frolics of the very highest came the gospel of smug, often aggressive puritanism. A doctrine was preached of sexual abstinence and of celibacy as a desired state. Even within marriage only the minimum sexual activity was allowable and then solely for the purpose of procreation and in no way was the activity to be enjoyed simply for its own sake!

Naturally, this suppressive attitude found a mirror image in the forthright celebration of sexuality that was reflected in the growth of underground magazines such as *The Oyster* or *Cremorne Gardens* that flourished during the last two decades of Queen Victoria's reign.

Many of the authors who contributed to these journals were journalists working on the fledgling popular newspapers that were burgeoning around this time.

Interestingly enough, the letters section of *The Oyster* were edited by Jenny Everleigh, whose own risqué diaries have recently been republished and Doctor Jonathan Arkley, who was called in privately by the Prince of Wales in 1892 to treat some unknown ailment that must have baffled the Royal Family's own physician Sir James Reid.

Doctor Arkley's 'Ask Doctor Jonathan' advice column was perhaps the most popular regular feature in the magazine. As Professor Alan Haley noted in his preface to *The Oyster 4* (New English Library, London 1989): 'Ignorance of even basic knowledge about sexuality was far more widespread than today and the agony column of Doctor Arkley provided a valuable conduit of information.'

The handsome young doctor was a leading light in the fast South Hampstead set whose members included Sir Ronnie Dunn, Sir Lionel Trapes and Colonel Cripps of the West Kents. But even his connections with the highest in the land could not save him from the consequences of seducing almost every pretty feminine patient who entered his surgery in Harley Street. After a cuckolded husband threatened to report him to the authorities, the randy doctor ceased practising and spent several years working in medical research in Europe and in the United States of America.

The letters to the editor of *The Oyster* (some written to Doctor Arkley and some simply penned for the delight of the writer and his or her reader) were often sent with instructions for a *nom de plume* to be printed, although several correspondents were happy to allow their full names and addresses to be published.

Perhaps, as Professor Cuthbertson of Glasgow suggests, the devotees of *The Oyster* believed themselves to be members of a loosely organised club and that members of the general public were excluded from this close, private circle. For so limited and exclusive was the circulation of this illicitly published magazine that the use of real names became a daring indulgence, a kind of curious private joke amongst the cognoscenti. And it is true that 'London Society' consisted of a very small group indeed. In his seminal work on horse racing in the latter half of the nineteenth century, Dr Loring Sayers estimates that all the people who 'mattered' in London could have fitted into the Prince of Wales' luxurious ballroom at his Marlborough House residence. And in the country as a whole, most of the political and social influence as well as wealth was concentrated in the hands of six or seven hundred land-owning families, many of which were closely interlinked through timely semi-arranged marriages.

It was a proud boast of *The Oyster* that all letters printed in its pages were uncensored and their contents are indeed explicit. This is bawdy writing without inhibition even by today's more liberal standards. Sexual adventure presses hard on the heels of sexual adventure and the sheer energy and variety of these frolics could become exhausting were it not for the high-spirited imagination and — more often perhaps in the case of the female scribes — frank and occasionally amusing wit displayed by the authors. This selection of letters shows that beneath those swelling but high-buttoned bodices, under that waistcoated, upright worthiness, there was an eager and inventive appetite for sexual pleasure, even in the most unlikely places.

For the social historian the letters pages of *The Oyster* show that the magazine provided a platform of resistance to the suffocating, guilt-ridden climate in which they first appeared. In the words of Antoinette Hillman-Strauss: "They set themselves firmly against the notion that sexuality was an area over which the Establishment should exercise a stringent, rigid control and this led to a more sceptical questioning attitude which in turn brought about the more relaxed and liberal philosophy that by and large exists today.

'Copies have fortunately survived to delight and amuse us as well as to provide an unusual and unconventional insight into the manners and mores of a vanished world, the reverse side to the coin of iron-clad respectability which appeared to characterise British society one hundred years ago.'

Godfrey Fulham
Nairobi
November, 1990

He who loves not wine, woman and song
Remains a fool his whole life long.

Attributed to Martin Luther

LETTERS TO THE EDITOR

From Colonel Leon Standlake

Sir,

Being a shareholder in the Mersey Railway Company, last week I accepted an invitation from the joint contractors of the Mersey Tunnel, Major Isaac of London and Waddells of Edinburgh, to descend the shafts of the tunnel and inspect the works beneath the river now that they have been practically completed. Readers may care to note that the excavations have amounted to more than twenty thousand cubic yards, all got out by hand.

The project was first mooted twenty-five years ago but the excavations have been dogged by many difficulties. However, since Professor William Bucknall's famous boring machine got to work three years ago, progress has been swift and very shortly the tunnel will be opened to the public.

Afterwards, along with a group of other major shareholders, I was invited to dine with the Lord Mayor of Liverpool at the Adelphi Hotel and stay the night at that august establishment as a guest of the Company. Naturally, after descending into the bowels of the earth, so to speak, I decided to run myself a bath before dinner. I began to undress but whilst pulling out my bathrobe from my valise I noticed that a handsomely bound book had been placed at the bottom of the bag. This was most curious as I had not instructed my valet, Stanley, to pack any reading material for me. I picked up the book and opened it to find that a card had been clipped onto the first pages.

11

Who could have sent this to me? I unclipped the plain white card which read: 'Leon, in case you get bored in Liverpool, I thought you may care to see the latest selection of French photographs just published by Monsieur Pierre Breslau of Paris. All best wishes − Rodney.' Now all was clear! You see, just a few days beforehand I had invited Sir Rodney Burbeck and his current amorata to spend a few days in London as my house guests, and the wealthy baronet must have surreptitiously smuggled this much-sought-after new book over from France. How kind of Rodney to give me a copy, I mused, as Monsieur Breslau's books are highly prized by the cognoscenti.

I sat down on the bed and browsed through the pages which were full of coloured photographs of the most lascivious evolutions of *l'arte de faire l'amour*. There were naked youths and girls with their cocks, pussies and bottoms displayed as they frigged, sucked and fucked in all kinds of varied positions. Perhaps my favourite was one of a most beautiful dark-skinned girl seated on the lap of her lover. Between her voluptuous thighs her cunt is seen delightedly engorged with his thick standing prick. Her arms are round his neck and her face is turned up, beaming with the satisfaction she is experiencing in her well-filled cunney.

Another showed a handsome couple dancing together, the boy pressing the soft bum cheeks of his partner who is holding his stiff prick in a tender, loving grasp. In the next plate the buxom beauty is shown lying nude on a bed, her legs apart with her splendid cunney protruding its full rounded lips from the midst of a covering of crisp curly hair, whilst the crimson crack between gives promise of a warm reception to his stiff standing prick which she has in her hand.

'I wouldn't mind taking his place for an hour or two,' I murmured to myself. And then I almost jumped out in shock! For a sweet feminine voice chimed out: 'And I wouldn't mind changing places with the girl either.'

I swivelled round to see who had entered my room unannounced and unbidden. No, it was not one of the sneak thieves who make a speciality of breaking into hotel bedrooms, but simply a very pretty young chambermaid, a slim young girl of no more than eighteen years of age, I judged, who sported a mane of long black hair, a pair of large blue eyes and a pretty retroussé nose.

She brushed back her hair sensuously as she said: 'Oh, I am so sorry to have startled you, Sir. I came in to turn down the bed but you failed to hear me.

'That must be a very absorbing book, Sir. May I have a look at it?' I nodded and the little minx sat down on the bed next to me and reached over to take the book. As she did so, her hand brushed against the bulge in my undershorts. 'She is a lucky girl,' said the maid softly. 'Just look at her aroused nipples, her luscious lips, she is just ready and waiting to be fucked.'

'I like the look of her too,' I said hoarsely and, before I could say anything more, this sweet girl pulled out my cock from my drawers and started pulling the swollen shaft up and down. Nothing loath, I unbuttoned her blouse and found that she was wearing nothing underneath! I began massaging her beautifully rounded breasts and then I pulled her skirt up with my other hand and soon we were locked in a passionate embrace.

'I've time for a quick one if you have,' she said softly, so lifting her in my arms I placed her on top of the bed. Soon we were fully nude and I started by sucking her breasts and massaging her clitty and pussey lips with my long fingers. I raised her legs and rested them on my shoulders as she directed my cock to her juicy pussey. I fucked her in my most favoured fashion, alternating slow and fast rhythms, responding to her thrusts. We were voyagers on a journey to the seventh heaven of fucking as I kissed her luscious lips and sucked her long, hard nipples. She exploded with multiple orgasms and my own pleasure was heightened by her moans and sighs. I pounded home the strokes faster and faster as we rocked together, climbing to almost unimaginable heights as my raging prick slid now uncontrollably in and out of her sopping love channel.

She moved excitedly under me as my prick jerked inside her and I could see by her wriggles of delight how much

13

she was enjoying this glorious surprise fuck and she panted: 'Oh Sir, how nice, how lovely, oh, how I am spending! I can feel my juices gushing. A-h-r-e, now, now, spunk into me!' I prolonged the pleasure for as long as possible, slowing down my thrusts to feel the delicious throbbings of cock and cunney in their perfect conjunction, but nature was not to be denied and I soon shot a copious stream of creamy white sperm inside her cunney as we swam in a mutual emission, both of us being so overcome by our feelings that we almost swooned in our ecstasy.

We would both have preferred to stay in bed for a repeat performance, but such a desire could not be granted as Sally (for we exchanged names after the fuck) had work to do and I could not excuse myself from attending the Lord Mayor's Dinner as I had accepted the invitation to propose the loyal toast.

I must note here what splendid fare we were offered at dinner. After a delicious thick vegetable soup I relished some excellent poached turbot followed by a selection of roasts: beef, mutton and fowl. But the highlight was a dessert of a succulent array of peaches, plums, apricots, nectarines, raspberries, strawberries, pears and grapes all grouped in generous pyramids among the flowers that adorned the buffet table.

So I was quite tired by the time I climbed into bed later that evening. I fell asleep almost immediately and I dreamed about fucking Sally again, sliding my cock into her wet pussey as I fondled her full breasts, and kissed her neck and shoulders from behind. Then I lay back and let the dear girl suck my cock to full erection before she mounted me.

Amazingly, awakening from my slumber, I realised that this was no dream! I was lying on my back and I could see and feel a girl bouncing up and down on my prick! I tried to speak and reached for the lamp but my lips were sealed with soft hands and a sweet little voice murmured: 'It's all right, it's only Sally. Everything is just fine.' Then she kissed me as she rode my cock and I fondled her stalky nipples, rubbing them to stiffness against the palms of my hands. Faster and faster she rode and as she cried out with joy,

14

she spent and I felt her warm love juices trickle down my shaft.

She started to gyrate her hips round and round and I grabbed her bum cheeks as I jerked upwards to meet her downward thrusts. Her lithe young body slipped up and down on my throbbing length, taking every last millimetre of my shaft deep into her pussey and the continuous nipping and contractions of her cunt soon brought me to a climax. I tried at first to hold back but I could feel the hot spunk boiling up in my balls and I crashed powerful jets of love juice up into her womb as she moved her hips faster and faster. The feel of her beautiful body rocking to and fro kept my cock hard even though I jetted spurt after spurt of spunk, filling her cunney with my cream. Gad! What an Elysian spend!

Yet still this highly sexed girl remained unsatisfied! She lay panting next to me, her long dark tresses shimmering in the moonlight that poured in through the window. She stretched and arched her back, caressing her pert young breasts and moving her legs suggestively as I placed my hand on her crisp, damp bush. I licked my lips and moved over to kiss her white belly and then ran my tongue lower, through the tickly pubic moss. My hands circled around her glorious bum cheeks as I buried my head between her thighs and drew her against me. My tongue found her glistening crack and she gasped and shivered as I found her clitty immediately and began to roll my tongue around the erectile piece of flesh.

'Oh! Oh! Leon, you suck clitty marvellously. That's gorgeous, gorgeous!' she cried out. 'Now let's try something else!' And with those words she wriggled herself onto her belly and twitched her rounded bum cheeks provocatively at me. Despite our previous exertions, my cock swelled up again at the sight of this lovely naked girl and I gave my shaft a little rub to bring it to its fullest stiffness.

Yet I hesitated for a moment as she pushed her bum upwards and opened her legs to give me a good view of her bum-hole. I looked at it for a moment and then placed my knob, which was still wet from our spendings, to the entrance of the puckered little rosette. 'Yes, yes, Leon,' she panted. 'Go on, go on, I want a nice thick length of cock up my bum. Go carefully though and we'll have a lovely bottom fuck.'

I angled her legs a little further apart to afford a better view of her little wrinkled nether orifice and gently eased my knob between her cheeks. At first I encountered a difficulty but then her sphincter muscle relaxed and I slid my cock in and out of the tight sheath, plunging in and out of the now widened rim as she reached back and spread her cheeks even further, jerking her bum in time to my rhythm as I wrapped one arm around her titties, frigging each of them in turn, and snaking my other arm round her waist I was able to finger-fuck her pussey to afford her a double pleasure.

Her bottom responded gaily to every shove as I drove home, my balls bouncing against her smooth rounded cheeks. I worked my proud prick in as far as it would go and I enjoyed a delicious tingling as I corked her to the very limit. I moved in and out as she worked her bum to bring me off in a flood of gushing spunk that both warmed and lubricated her delicious backside. As I spurted into her I continued to work my prick back and forth so that it remained stiffly hard until, with an audible plop, I withdrew from her well-lathered sheath.

'That was very nice indeed, Sally,' I said with genuine solicitude. 'I always worry a little about suggesting a bottom fuck myself as unless performed with care it can be painful for the lady.'

'Thank you for being so thoughtful, my dear. I wouldn't like to be cornholed every day but it makes a pleasant change now and then,' she smiled. 'Do you know something, I am rather thirsty. Now I hope you will excuse the impertinence but I took the liberty of ordering a bottle of iced champagne to be sent to your room. I brought it up myself and I hope you don't mind too much.'

'Of course not, Sally! So long as it's a good vintage,' I laughed.

Now the champagne (a Moet and Chandon '82)

invigorated me to a further bout which began with a lovely kiss and cuddle. We lay in a comfortable *soixante neuf* with Sally's thighs clasped round my head and her spunk-coated pussey lips pressed firmly against my mouth. As I licked up the morsels of our previous repast, she sucked my cock up to yet another fine erection and licked around that ultra-sensitive area between my arsehole and my balls. Then she moved her wicked little tongue up my cockshaft to my helmet, flicking at it with the very tip so expertly that I could feel my balls tightening and my prick swelling up to a rock-like hardness.

I slowly entered her until my prick was in to the hilt and I stayed still a moment, savouring to the full the delicious little contractions of her cunt as it welcomed my cock into its portals. I don't think I have ever experienced a more soothing, moist, warm home for my throbbing prick.

We started moving together and Sally treated me to a long, slow fuck as I glided my shaft in and out of her pulsating pussey. Then we raised the tempo and our lips meshed together as our bottoms began to work in unison. How tightly her cunt enclasped and sucked upon my prick! We gloried in each giant thrust as her juices dripped onto my balls as they banged against her bum. She implored me to drive deeper by twirling her tongue in my mouth and, cupped now in my broad palms, her bum cheeks rotated eagerly as my trusty tool rammed in and out and she cried out with joy at the stinging excitement of my thick prick driving furiously into her soft depths. I felt the white froth spurt upwards and Sally gave a little yelp of pleasure as the hot creamy spunk flooded and I felt her shudder as she drained me of every last drop of love juice.

She let my now limp tool slide out of her before covering me with kisses and we fell exhausted into a deep sleep. Luckily Sally was not on duty until two o'clock the next day for we did not wake up until half past eight in the morning. In order to keep our assignment secret from the hotel management, we shared the large breakfast that I ordered to be sent up to my room and Sally hid in the bathroom when it was brought in.

Although she asked for nothing (except the use of my cock!), I insisted on leaving her a present of ten guineas in gratitude for making my stay in Liverpool so pleasant, which after first demurring to take, she accepted, thanking me heartily for my generosity.

Now, Sir, my old friend Sir Robert Dixon has chided me for leaving 'such a trifling sum' whilst Mr Peter Stockman of Sevenoaks insists I was wrong to even offer any money at all! I would be most interested to read your comments upon this matter.

I am, Sir, Your Obedient Servant

Colonel Leon Standlake
Goldstone House
Cramley
Near Stafford
March, 1885

The Editor replies: The general consensus in our office is that your behaviour was beyond reproach. It is easy for Mr Stockman to criticise for it is well known that certain ladies pay him large amounts of cash for their weekly fuckings. But then, is there a man in Britain who can equal the length and girth of Mr Stockman's extraordinary organ? He occasionally is guilty of forgetting his good fortune.

From Miss Anna Curkin-Nayland

Sir,

Like the poet I too best enjoy the 'season of mists and mellow fruitfulness' and I trust your readers will find to their liking this completely true tale of autumnal lechery in which I must confess my involvement. Well now, perhaps 'confess' is the wrong word to use for I am not in the least ashamed at what took place. In the words of Mr Sheridan, 'certainly nothing is unnatural that is not physically impossible' and I would be happy to submit to your judgement of my admittedly lewd behaviour.

Last Wednesday I decided to take a post-prandial constitutional stroll through Hyde Park. It was a fine if slightly chilly afternoon but I enjoyed my unhurried walk, listening to the first thrushes singing and watching a group of starlings swarming around a clump of crab apple trees, pecking wastefully at the ripe fruit. Leaves were still to be found lingering in some trees — deep, shiny yellow on the birches, pale green and golden on the elms.

I was so engrossed by the beauties of nature that I failed to notice that a girl who was walking in front of me had stopped to deposit an unwanted newspaper in a litter bin and a slight collision ensued.

'Oh, I do beg your pardon,' I gasped. 'How very foolish of me, I was simply not looking where I was going.'

'That's alright, Anna, no damage done,' said the girl cheerfully. 'It's just as well though that you were not at the wheel of one of these new horseless carriages or a really nasty accident could have ensued.'

How did she know my name? I looked at her closely and

although I recognised the voice, I could not quite place the face of this extremely attractive blonde-haired blue-eyed creature who giggled and said: 'I do believe that you have forgotten who I am. Mind, it must be four or five months ago since we dined together at my cousin Jenny Everleigh's house in South Audley Street, Mayfair, a few days before I sailed to New York.'

Suddenly my memory returned. 'Of course I remember you! Your name is Molly Farquhar, Jenny's cousin from Cockfosters in Hertfordshire. What a nice surprise to meet you again. Yes, I recall your telling me that you spend a great deal of time in America. When did you come back home, Molly?'

'I returned last week as my Mama insists that it is time for me to "settle down" and look for a suitable husband. As she says, *ad nauseum*, you are now twenty-two Molly and we don't want you left on the shelf! Aren't parents difficult!'

'Well, mine are away in France until November. But tell me, Molly, have you any beaux in England? I have just ended a friendship with Benjamin, Sir Ronnie Dunn's son, as although we enjoyed each other's company very much, neither of us wishes to make a commitment in respect of a permanent relationship. So I suppose I am on the look-out myself for male friendship.

'Ah, you poor love. Have you been saddened by the ending of the affair? I hear from my cousin Jenny that Sir Ronnie wields a good stiff prick but I don't know whether his son is as good a cocksman as his father.'

I was somewhat shocked at her forthright speech but I was determined not to appear unsophisticated and replied: 'Oh, Ben could fuck very passably. He was a most gentle and considerate lover and his prick was always up to the mark.'

'That's good to know for a hard man is good to find. One so often comes across those who after just one spend can no longer raise any further interest, which can be most unsatisfactory, particularly if one has not yet spent oneself,' commented Molly as we continued our stroll together. 'Tell me, though, Anna, have you ever experienced the joys of female-only fucking? I can thoroughly recommend it as it makes a very pleasant change which I know from my own personal experience.'

'Not since some horseplay in the sixth form dormitory of Lady Bracknell's Academy for Young Ladies,' I said doubtfully. 'I think it would take a lot to persuade me that it could rival the benefits of a hot, stiff cock in my cunney, a joy that surely cannot be bettered.'

Molly laughed and said 'I used to think like that but since I joined Lady Slapbum's Ting Tong Club in Redcliffe Gardens, I have changed my mind about tribadism. Look, if you have no appointments this afternoon, let's hail a hansom and I'll show you round the place for as a country member I am entitled to sign in up to three guests per month. In any case, they serve a delicious tea at the Ting Tong which you will enjoy whatever you think of the goings-on at the club. I always try and smuggle out a slice of Mrs Bickler's sponge for my current beau and pretend that I made it.'

[*The Ting Tong Club flourished between 1888 and 1899 when its flourishing membership was threatened by exposure following a police raid. Although lesbianism was not, per se, illegal the Club's owners were charged with keeping a disorderly house. However, as its members included those from amongst the highest ranks of Society, the matter was swiftly hushed up. Nevertheless, the Club was forced to close and the house was bought by Professor Taylor Cuthbertson, a close friend of the Prince of Wales* — *Editor*.]

My diary was free of engagements so I accepted her kind invitation. We were fortunate enough to find a cab almost immediately and within ten minutes we were at the entrance of the club. Molly insisted on paying the driver and we climbed the stairs to the front door. An attractive young girl dressed in a rather scanty maid's uniform opened the door and took our coats as I signed my name in the visitors' book.

'Are there no footmen?' I asked Molly quietly. 'An establishment such as this should really boast a butler or some other male flunkey.'

'Are you joking?' whispered Molly. 'Why, they wouldn't even let a eunuch or a nancy-boy darken its doors. They say that even Lady Slapbum's Pekinese is a bitch! Anyhow, let me show you round the club.'

It certainly was a luxuriously appointed house with rich fittings in every room. All amenities one would expect to find were provided — a lounge, card-room, dining room etc., although smoking was not permitted except in the billiards room as a majority of the members disliked the smell of tobacco.

'There are a number of bedrooms upstairs for the use of members,' said Molly brightly. 'Shall we take a look?'

I somehow guessed that we would be staying a while upstairs, but I allowed myself to be shepherded aloft and Molly pushed open the door of the room on the right at the top of the stairs. 'Take a look at this bedroom, Anna,' said Molly, inviting me inside. 'See, through there is the bathroom and Lady Slapbum has installed these new showers which I find most invigorating.'

'Really,' I said with interest. 'Do you prefer using them as opposed to taking a bath?'

'Well, I always enjoy a nice soak in a warm tub but these new showers do tone one up as well as cleansing the grime of the city from the skin. One can adjust the hot and cold taps so that the water comes through at just the right temperature. Look, I will call down and see if we can try it out here and now.'

Her call on the internal telephone system was quickly answered and she gaily informed me that the room was ours for the next two hours. We undressed in an unhurried manner and I followed Molly into the bathroom where she switched on this new-fangled equipment, and after putting on special caps for our hair, we splashed around together underneath the warm water that cascaded down on top of us. Afterwards we dried ourselves on the large soft towels provided and Molly curled herself up sensuously on the bed.

I must admit that I had already noticed her superb figure and I envied her golden blonde locks of hair as I have always been firmly of the opinion that gentlemen prefer blondes.

Nevertheless, although her firm uptilted breasts were well proportioned, I judged that mine were larger and my legs were perhaps slightly longer than hers. At the base of her flat tummy there was conclusive evidence that Molly was indeed a genuine blonde for her silky pussey hair was also that fine shade of gold which I so envied, although my own black bush has been the object of admiration from not only young Benjamin Dunn but by such well-known cocksmen as Gordon McChesney, David Haines and Colonel Philip Pelham of the Lancashire Fusiliers.

Molly was leafing through a copy of *Cremorne Gardens* and I leaned over to see if there was anything worth reading in this naughty publication. 'Come and lie down with me and read out one of these stories. I do love listening to lewd tales,' said Molly invitingly, patting the snowy white sheet with her hand.

I obediently lay down beside her, snuggling my head inside the welcoming crook of her arm, and began to read from a story by Madame Estelle de Quentonne, the famous French courtesan who is reputed often to entertain the Prince of Wales when he makes one of his frequent visits to Paris. However, in the tale from which I read, she was writing of an enjoyable little joust with Claude, the sixteen-year-old nephew of Eduard Raspis, the industrial magnate. I began: 'My lips were drawn as if by an invisible magnet to the mushroom dome of Claude's lovely young cock. I kissed the smooth, hot head and thoroughly wet the top as I opened my mouth and took in the glistening knob, lashing my tongue around the succulent sweetmeat. Ah, it tasted so masculine, with a fresh salty tang that I closed my lips around it as tightly as possible and worked on the tip with my tongue, easing my lips forward to take more of the shaft. In his eagerness he pushed my head down to take in more of his throbbing tool but I almost choked in doing so.

'He retracted slightly so that it lay motionless though pulsating inside my mouth. I closed my lips around this monster and moved my tongue across its width. I sucked greedily on his youthful cock and twisted his head down so that his face was pushed into my own sopping groin and my body shook with delight as the clever lad realised what he had to do and began to circle his tongue around my dripping slit.'

It may have been inappropriate to read such a tale inside the Ting Tong Club but it certainly aroused myself and Molly who was by now idly running her cool hands up and down my thighs and, combined with the stimulating story I was reading, we were both soon squirming around on the bed. She took the magazine from me and threw it on the carpet and leaning over me, she kissed me fully on the lips before transferring her tongue to my ear which set shivers all through my body, especially when she started to press my titties between her fingers which intensified the tingling sensations tremendously.

By now my whole body was shaking with lust and when Molly began stroking my pussey I grasped her hand and pushed it firmly between my legs which I squeezed together, crushing her hand between them. She understood my urgent need for she let her head slide down from my ear to my tummy and into my black thatch of pussey hair. She parted my lips with her fingers and slipped her tongue into my wet cunney, licking all round the edge with the tip before thrusting it all the way in. She was teasing my pussey to unbelievable heights, using tongue and fingers to spread my wetness all round my cunt. I just closed my eyes and let myself dissolve into a glorious sea of lubricity as her teeth now nibbled along my cunney lips whilst her pink little tongue teased my clitty with long, rasping licks. Up and down, in and out her long tongue lapped up my slippery juices as, by now totally abandoned, I threw my legs high up upon her shoulders.

Now I could feel myself begin to experience the first sensations of a spend build up inside me. 'Oh, Anna, your juices taste so delicious. I love sucking your juicy cunney,' gasped Molly, diving back again to give me the final *coup de grace*. She lashed her tongue against my clitty, rubbing it until it stuck out between my lips. Then she wrenched her mouth from my sopping muff and replaced it with her fingers, finding my swollen clitty which she tugged only for a few seconds before I was away! My body thrashed wildly about in a frenzied ecstasy as her finger slid into my bum-hole. I exploded into uncontrollable spasms of excitement and my juices flowed freely as I reached a gigantic peak of orgasmic lust.

Molly and I writhed about in each others arms, our breasts crushed together, our tawny titties rubbing against each other as we kissed feverishly until a second eruption made me arch back again, almost crying with joy as the raging storm of my spend coursed through me.

Now it was my turn to make Molly spend and she laid back expectantly as I kissed her stalky red nipples with their saucer like brown aureoles, drawing circles with my tongue, flicking the nipples up to a ripe hardness. Then I kissed her belly all the way down to that soft, golden nest . . .

Dipping my face close so that I could nuzzle into that silky blonde pussey, I licked my fingers and separated her folds, inhaling the tangy feminine odour of her dripping slit. Spreading her lips with my tongue, I explored her sopping pussey, gauging her responses, then sliding my arms around her thighs I adjusted my position and relaxed into flowing movements with my head, my tongue nudging her clitty, pushing against the hood. Her pelvis set the tempo, coming to meet me faster and faster as I increased the speed, pressing down with my teeth as she began to toss from side to side.

'Oh, Anna, that's marvellous. Oh yes, oh yes! Now darling, finger me,' she panted. 'Finish me off with your fingers.' She put her hands on her inner thighs and pulled her legs apart, revealing her fleshy pink outer lips. She was so swollen and wet that she hardly noticed three of my fingers slide into her sopping cunney. But she certainly did when I started to work up a pacey rhythm, working my fingers in and out, slowly at first, then faster and faster as she got wetter and wetter. She now frigged her clitty at the same time, working the little rosebud around with her thumb and forefinger. I straddled her and whilst I jerked one hand in and out of her pussey I roughly tweaked her titties with the other, making her moan with pleasure as she spent profusely, shrieking so loudly with delight that I was afraid we might be disturbed.

Well, dear readers, we were indeed disturbed — but not by any outraged members of the Ting Tong Club. What we had failed to hear in our haste to enjoy each other's bodies was the sound of a ladder being placed against the window and the thwack of the window cleaner's shoes as he climbed up the rungs to undertake his duties. It was Molly who first discovered that we had been performing in front of an audience. She suddenly shot out of bed and grabbed a towel to cover herself as she padded towards the window.

'Anna, look outside, we have an unannounced guest!' said Molly fiercely, opening the window to drag in a young man of about twenty-three who was still clutching his washleather. 'Shall I call Lady Slapbum and tell her that we have a Peeping Tom or —'

'Oh please don't do that,' said the young man who spoke in a far more educated voice than one would have expected from a London workman. 'I'm only doing the job because the regular window cleaner is ill and my aunt, Mrs Norma Swaige, who lives next door told me to offer my services to Lady Slapbum with whom she plays bridge every Wednesday afternoon. I had no idea this room was occupied but I must admit that when I saw what was going on, I was transfixed and just could not bring myself to move away.'

'Yes, I thought you were a member of the leisured classes as your face is quite familiar,' I mused, quite forgetting that I was sitting up in bed stark naked in front of this handsome young man who was now engaged in the most fulsome of apologies for looking in on our love-making.

'My name is Richard Gewirtz,' said the handsome youth with a slight bow. 'My father is Count Gewirtz of Galicia and though he never married my mother he immediately settled ten thousand a year and a London house upon her when I was born and he has kindly allowed me to bear his name.'

'I know your father,' said Molly promptly. 'He is a very kind gentleman as you rightly say. Why, after fucking my cousin Jenny Everleigh he insisted upon sending her first

26

class tickets for herself and a friend to travel to New York upon the Dutch liner *S. S. Rotterdam*.'

'Well, it wasn't all that kind,' admitted Richard with a short laugh. 'After all, he does own sixty per cent of the Trans Europe Shipping Line and he gets more free tickets than he knows what to do with.'

'Still, he need not have offered them to Jenny,' smiled Molly who was now mollified by Richard's forthright explanation and apology.

'Meanwhile, I have an excellent idea. You can make up for your intrusion by lending us your cock for the next thirty minutes. I have a great fancy for a fuck whilst I am sure that Anna would also be interested in seeing what you have to offer and whether you can use your tool half as well as your dear Papa,' she added.

He blushed shyly and said: 'Nothing would please me more but I feel so nervous that I don't know whether I will be able to — '

'Oh don't worry about all that, we'll get you in the mood, have no fear. Now you go and undress and take a quick shower. When you come back we will be ready for you,' commanded Molly.

Richard stripped off and I stole a quick look at his hairy, muscular torso, his well-made legs and tight little bottom as he made his way to the bathroom.

Meanwhile Molly clambered back onto the bed, but this time she leaned over and took out a wooden box standing upon the bedside table before wrapping an arm around me. 'This is a Ting Tong dildo box,' she explained. 'Let's hunt around and find something to play with whilst Richard gets ready.' It didn't take long for us to discover a superbly fashioned ivory double-ended godamiche which we put into immediate use. Molly lay back and pushed one end into her soft, sticky pussey. I lay with my legs through hers and positioned myself on the other end of the dildo. What a great feeling it was, cunt-to-cunt with a dear friend and with a nice thick staff inside me. We rocked back and forth together, enjoying the wonderful feeling of rigidity inside us. I love that sensation of having something hard and stiff pushing up inside me, filling me up whilst my cunney juices flow all around it. It was extremely stimulating although of course it could not really rival the hot, throbbing hardness of a genuine cock.

Richard came back into the room as we finished our spree. Neither of us had actually come but our pussies were now well juiced up and ready for a male intruder. 'Come and join us, there's no need to be shy,' I said, as the young man still held back. He smiled and dropping the towel which was draped around his waist, he walked towards us. He certainly was blessed with a thick stalk between his legs, but though it was swinging heavily, it was far from being ready for business but as I judged at the time, he only needed a little encouragement to light the fire.

For how quickly things changed when we got Richard onto the bed between us. We rolled him over on to his back and I sat across his knees while Molly sat perched on his chest. I took hold of his prick in my hand and it immediately swelled up under my soft touch. I knelt down and rubbed my breasts and nipples over his stiff shaft and then took the gleaming helmet into my mouth and began sucking noisily upon it as Molly moved up to place her pussey over his mouth so that he could tongue her cunney. Molly was making throaty noises as his tongue probed inside her cunney lips. His now huge prick was more than a mouthful for me as I sucked away on his knob, caressing his shaft until it was as stiff as iron. Then I shifted myself and lowered my lubricated cunt over his pulsating penis. I sank down gratefully, feeling the ivory column penetrate deeper and deeper inside me. Molly and I bounced up and down on poor Richard in unison and together we wriggled atop our young stud and I could feel waves of arousal taking me over.

After a minute or two of this treatment he removed his face from Molly's pussey and let out a loud growl. I felt his cock throb wildly and shoot out a rivulet of frothy white spunk as he spent copiously, the hot love juice filling my cunney and running down my thighs. A considerate and thoughtful man, Richard recovered himself enough to keep stimulating Molly's pussey with his tongue while his fingers now sought my clitty to finish me off. Molly came quite quickly and he lapped up her love juices as she spent copiously over his face.

'I can't get there without a cock in my cunt,' I said regretfully as I did not believe that Richard was capable of raising any interest for a while. But happily he proved me wrong as the young sportsman simply gave his cock a swift shake and I was amazed to see it swell up to its former flagpole-like state. I took hold of it in my hand and found that such was the girth that I needed two hands to grasp the thick pole. Molly made way for me to lie on my back and Richard threw himself across me. He took his monster cock in one hand and drove home. I could feel it stretching my muscles beyond any previous capacity and I experienced a fulfilment that was simply divine and the thought flashed through my mind that as nice as the little tribadistic episode had been with Molly, nothing could beat the sensation of a big fat prick up one's cunney. Ah, what bliss! Every millimetre of my nook tingled to the pumping of his surging shaft as his wrinkled hairy ballsack bounced against my bum.

'Oh, you big-cocked boy! Fuck my juicy cunt with your thick prick!' I panted as he thrust home, sliding his shaft in and out of my squelchy wetness.

Several times I thought he was on the point of spunking yet somehow he held back until I was ready for him. Again and again, faster and faster he pounded in and out of my crack until my lips emitted one long, hoarse wail as I climaxed again and again in a seemingly multiple orgasm.

Then suddenly he pulled out and reared over me. He gripped his prick hard, giving it two or three convulsive jerks until a huge squirt of salty sperm spouted out, arcing towards my breasts, splashing my nipples, streaming down my belly and into my curly bush.

'Oh, how lewd!' gasped Molly who was watching avidly, frigging herself unashamedly with her hand as she watched me rub the spunk around my erect nipples and all over my belly.

29

'I haven't finished yet, Anna,' grunted this son of Count Gewirtz, one of the most famous fuckers in Europe. 'Let me show you how I earned my soubriquet of "the gobbling Galician".'

For yes, dear readers, young Richard Gewirtz's cock was still standing stiff as he knelt back between my legs and slipped his rigid rod back into my soaking slit. Frankly, I just could not keep up and whispered that my pussey could not take too much more cock without a rest. Being a gentleman he replaced his thick prick with his soft, caressing tongue which soothed my sore pussey. He moved round so that his cock was dangling over my face and I took it immediately into my mouth, sucking hard on it. I flicked my tongue against the ridge of his helmet, moving my lips from balls to tip and back again, faster and faster, intoxicated perhaps by the rhythm we had set up.

Suddenly I felt that warm ripple begin in my womb and at the same time his tight buttocks jerked and his great cock shoved hard against the back of my throat. Then his hot frothy flood was released and I felt it spurting out as I greedily swallowed all his love juice, milking that lovely prick until the last drops had been drained from him.

When we had recovered we discussed a plan for Richard to visit us when he was next in Mayfair (for the lad was currently living in Islington) and he exited from the room through the window and down the ladder to the ground.

'Lucky for us that Lady Slapbum will never get to hear of what happened here this afternoon,' commented Molly, 'or I would be expelled from the Club.'

We talked about our three-in-a-bed frolic over tea and I maintained that despite my enjoyment of being finger-fucked by Molly, I still preferred boys as, shall we say, the main course as compared to the girls who could provide a dessert. If a choice were imposed, I would happily live on the meat and easily forgo the pudding — especially if all the cocks measured up to that of Richard Gewirtz.

So ended a grand afternoon's fucking, Mr Editor, but now I must ask you — was I too forward in accepting Molly's invitation to take part in lesbian love and should we perhaps have simply ignored our randy young window cleaner who may have only fucked us both out of politeness?

Your humble scribe,

Anna Curkin-Nayland
69 Laurie Mansions
Kensington Gore
London, W.
July, 1891

The Editor replies: I am sure that all our readers agree that you deserved your enjoyment. One must experience as many of the joys placed before us by a beneficient Creator as possible or we could be accused of scorning his gifts.

As Mr Coleridge has it:
All thoughts, all passions, all delights.
Whatever stirs this mortal frame,
All are but minister of Love,
And feed his sacred flame.

I do hope that you continue to enjoy an active and varied love-life.

From Mr Stanley Wright

Sir,

One of the most stringent areas of control exercised by our so-called 'betters' has been that of human sexuality. It is drummed into us that all sexual expression, other than the minimum required for the purposes of procreation, are 'bad' and we ourselves are somehow sinful if we 'pander' to those normal deep-seated biological drives.

Of course, there must be rules and regulations for the conduct of civilised sexual relations. Men who force themselves upon unwilling partners — both inside and outside marriage — are worth little more than the beasts of the field and deserve the harshest of punishments.

However, there can surely be no harm in fantasising about fucking and I must admit that if, for example, I were fortunate enough to be dining with Miss Jenny Everleigh, the scenario would unfold in the following fashion . . .

After a sumptuous repast in my London *pied à terre* in Dyott Street, Bloomsbury, I would slip under the table and gently kiss her knees until she relaxed. I would lift her skirt and continue kissing her legs, gradually working higher and higher, my tongue making wet tracks on her soft inner thighs.

When I reached the edge of her brief knickers I would breathe deeply to inhale her pungent feminine odour and then I would place my lips on the crotch of her knickers and blow gently, my warm breath causing Jenny's pussey to become damper and even more fragrant. She would then wriggle her delicious bottom to assist me in pulling down her knickers so that I could nuzzle my face into her silky pubic bush. I would then kiss those pouting pussey lips and, spreading them apart I would alternately drive my tongue deep into her cunney and then pull out to tickle her clitty with small flicks of the tip of my tongue. Finally, I would suck upon that hard button until she gasped with pleasure and flooded my mouth with her tangy love juice.

We would then move to the bed where we would undress each other and she would lay down on the sheet, her eyes gleaming with anticipation as I fondle her breasts and suck the nipples up to a delightful erection. Then I would slip first one finger and then several into her cunt, playfully rubbing her engorged clitty. Occasionally, I would slip my sopping fingers out and let her lick off the salty wetness.

My cock would now be throbbing as Jenny stroked it and gently squeezed my balls. She would smile at the way my hot, hard prick would leap around in her hand and then she would slip down and lap at the fiery red helmet before tonguing my shaft and giving each of my balls a little suck. She would then transfer her attention back to my knob, lapping her wet tongue around the 'eye' before taking my prick into her soft mouth, her wet lips straining to encircle it, finally sliding juicily up and down my pulsating prick until she sucked it deep into her throat, all the way up to my balls.

Somehow, I would manage to turn round into a 'sixty-nine' so that my face was level with her pussey and I would lap up and down her lips, pulling them apart with my fingers so that I could concentrate on her erect little clitty. She gasps with joy and cries out: 'Yes, yes! You're so good. Keep sucking! Eat my pussey! Oh, how I adore it!' and I flick her clitty harder until she spends, her hips bucking as her juices soak my lips.

It is all that I can do not to spend myself, but I manage to maintain my composure as we separate and she would raise her knees and spread them, inviting me to implant my cock into her warm, private love hole. I move up and place her legs on top of my shoulders as I bend down to kiss her. I rub the head of my cock against her soaking crack and slowly I sink into her gorgeous cunt. I pull out and re-enter; each stroke brings me slightly deeper and she whispers fiercely: 'Fuck me, Stanley! Fuck me! What a huge cock you have and how divinely you use it!' Thrusting deep into her dripping pussey I feel her cunney grasping my cock as I slide into the hilt. Her slick channel clasps my shaft lovingly with each long, slow stroke. My hands are roving around her fabulous breasts and she cries: 'Tit-fuck me, darling! There's a good boy! Squirt your spunk on my lovely nips!'

As always, I am ready to please a lady so I pull out of her cunt and she wraps her big breasts around my cock. I thrust between the jiggling flesh and with every stroke she kisses the crown of my cock . . .

It is too much and I finally erupt with wads of white sperm shooting out of my cock and she opens her mouth and catches some to swallow. She takes hold of my throbbing shaft and sucks it feverishly, milking my prick of every last drop of frothy juice.

Time is closing in on us so once my cock has hardened up again (with a little help from Jenny's friendly tongue), I am ready to fuck her pussey and she turns on her hands and knees and, raising her tight little rounded bottom cheeks, begs me to fuck her doggy-style. I guide it into her sopping slit from behind, my knob sliding easily between her cunney lips and she thrusts her bottom out as I pump forward, locking us into a sensuous rhythm as my thick, stiff shaft rams in and out of her soaking crack. But all too soon I can feel the hot sperm bubble up in my balls and up through my prick which is now thrusting at speed in and out of Jenny's delightful passion pit. I let out a cry of warning and then wham! I plunge my trusty tool as far into her cunney as possible and my balls bang against her bum cheeks as the gorgeous girl thrusts back her bum to receive the spurts of spunk that shoot out from my cock.

Alas, she cannot stay the night and we bathe and dress for she must return home before midnight or risk the wrath of her Mama. Ah, if only I could but translate a fond fantasy into a glorious reality, at the end of my days I would enter the fields of Elysium.

Yours sincerely,

Stanley Wright
Stamford Bridge
York
September, 1892

The Editor replies: I have taken the liberty of sending your billet doux to Miss Everleigh who is spending the summer in the Lake District with Lord Goulthorpe. She asks me to convey her sincere regards but regrets that she is currently being fucked by Sir Graham Giddens and cannot entertain any further pricks until further notice. Nevertheless, she was most flattered that she was the object of desire in your spellbinding fantasy. She is in possession of your name and address, and if the occasion ever arises that she finds herself in Yorkshire, be assured that she will contact you.

From The Honourable Lawrence Judd-Hughes

Sir,

This cautionary tale will demonstrate the necessity of keeping an accurate appointments diary.

Last Thursday evening I invited three friends from my Club round to my apartments for a few rubbers of bridge. For the record, these gentlemen are probably known to many readers of *The Oyster*; Sir Lionel Trapes, the *bon viveur* and Permanent Financial Secretary at The Treasury; Captain Jock Gibson of Edinburgh and Mr John Walsh, the noted author and critic.

As I shepherded my guests into the lounge, I instructed my man, Bacon, to put a magnum of champagne on ice and bring it in when the bottle had chilled.

'Very good, Sir,' said Bacon who then, instead of retiring with our hats and coats, laid his hand on my arm and hissed: 'Sir, I hope you will not mind my reminding you that you have a *rendez-vous* tonight with Lady Paula Platts-Lane. I could not help but overhear your telephone conversation with her the other morning.'

'By Gad, Bacon, it had completely slipped my mind. I was going to take her to some wretched concert this evening at the Wigmore Hall. Damn, damn, damn! I can't even contact her as she's spending the afternoon with friends out of town.'

'What shall I do, Sir?'

'Well, she said she would take a Prestoncrest carriage and meet me here at eight o'clock, but if she was delayed she would simply come round here as soon as possible and we would spend the evening quietly together.'

'Let's hope she is so engrossed with her friends that she decides to forgo the pleasures of the concert,' said Bacon hopefully. 'After all it is only a charity affair tonight put on by Lady Valerie Fitzcockie of Finchley, and so long as you have bought the seats it hardly matters whether or not they are occupied.'

'That's true enough,' I said. 'Nevertheless, at best I shall still have to explain to Paula that we will be unable to dine *à deux* as I promised. She will be very angry, to say the least.'

'But so long as you fuck her, Sir, I am sure that she will be satisfied,' murmured Bacon.

I smiled briefly and ordered him to announce Lady Paula and to show her into the lounge whenever she made an appearance. I then followed my guests inside, mixed them some hearty drinks and we sat down to enjoy our game, though I warned them that I had <u>forgotten</u> my previous arrangement with my current *amorata*.

As it so happens, Paula did not arrive until nearly nine o'clock so that in any case we would have been unable to attend Lady Fitzcockie's concert.

Bacon brought in some sandwiches and champagne, which went down perhaps a little too well as between us we managed to finish the best part of two bottles of my best Scotch whisky even before we began to eat. I freely admit that I was having a slight problem distinguishing spades from clubs and diamonds from hearts for frankly, I have never been a great imbiber and am unable to consume the vast amounts of alcohol that Messrs Walsh and Gibson, for example, can enjoy without any apparent ill-effects.

I well remember, however, that I was dealing out the cards when Bacon threw open the door and announced the arrival of Lady Paula Platts-Lane. I rose somewhat unsteadily to greet her along with the other three gentlemen and I apologised most profusely for having double-booked the evening.

'Oh, don't worry, Larry,' said Paula brightly. 'We would never have been able to go to the concert and I'm quite tired with all the talking this afternoon. You see, some of us girls

37

are going to start up a ladies' club in Belgravia to rival some of your wretched men-only institutions.'

'I trust you do not plan to exclude men from this new establishment,' commented John Walsh, his eyes roving over Paula's wavy brown hair, her attractive face, slim figure, well rounded, firm breasts and long, shapely legs. 'Alas, our club committee will not countenance a lady being introduced into the place.'

'No, we are not so blinkered as the members of the Rawalpindi,' smiled Paula. 'Men will be allowed inside our club, but strictly by invitation only.'

I finished dealing the cards but none of us made to pick any up. Like my three friends I was staring unashamedly at Paula's cream-coloured blouse which was made of such a flimsy material that it was quite transparent and we could easily make out the outline of her large, heavy breasts for she was wearing nothing underneath it, and despite my somewhat dazed state, my prick began to stir as I gazed upon her dark, swollen nipples that pressed against their thin covering.

Paula knew full well what we were staring at but she said nothing except to tell us to finish our game. Slowly and unwillingly we picked up our cards and tried hard to concentrate upon bridge and to banish the sight of Paula's titties from our brains. It was a most difficult feat to accomplish and Sir Lionel, who is generally considered to be amongst the best players in London, unnecessarily trumped John Walsh's winning ten of diamonds whilst I foolishly neglected to cover Jock Gibson's queen of hearts with the king. In normal circumstances such plays would have brought forth cries of rage from the wronged partners, but our minds were no longer on the game.

Indeed, play slowed to a complete halt when Paula said: 'Hasn't it been a warm day, gentlemen? Larry, you do keep this room far too warm. I do declare that you must have also forgotten to instruct Bacon not to light a fire in the hearth.'

With a gleam in his eye Sir Lionel suggested that perhaps she might like to take off some clothes. '*Some* clothes,

Lionel?' echoed Jock Gibson. 'All of them, more like. How about it, Paula?'

She said nothing but looked the gallant Scottish soldier straight in the eye as she undid the buttons on her blouse and slowly peeled it off. If Bacon was listening at the keyhole (a habit which is endemic in many servants) he must have heard the collective intake of breath as we were given full view of her nude breasts that jutted out proudly, the large titties pouting lasciviously as she caressed her delicious globes, rubbing the nipples up to a stalky firmness.

Then she quickly undid her ankle-length skirt and we gasped as she let it fall to the floor. She was wearing only the briefest of frilly lace knickers and after she stepped out of the skirt which lay on my Persian carpet, she sidled up to Jock and in a tantalising whisper said to him: 'Well, Jock, do you like what you see? Is your Caledonian cock rising in your drawers? If you'll pull down my knickers I'll show you that even an empty whisky bottle has its uses for a clever girl.'

'This promises to be interesting if my guess at what Paula has in mind is correct,' grinned Sir Lionel lewdly.

'Wait and see,' she replied throatily. 'Larry, be an angel and play a little light music on the piano to get me in the mood.'

You are already in the mood, Paula, I thought to myself as I acceded to her request. What should I play? Brahms, perhaps, or maybe Lizst? No, let it be Beethoven, I decided as I knew how fond she was of his music. I struck up the chords of the beautiful Appassionata and this certainly set Paula off. She danced sensuously around the room before sitting on the sofa with the empty bottle in her hand. Then she slowly leaned backwards, her legs pressed tightly together and she caressed the neck of the bottle with her lips and tongue. Then she moved it lower, running it over her breasts and snow-white tummy before moving it even lower to cut a path through her thick brown bush of curly hair at the base of her belly.

Then she moaned and opened her legs so that we saw her

39

pouting pink pussey lips appear and she moved the bottle between them, pressing the neck gently into her pussey, frigging herself off with it, sliding it in and out of her dampening cunney. This stimulating sight sent Jock Gibson's blood boiling and in a trice he had stripped naked, and holding his stiff shaft in his hand he padded over to the couch. He leaned over Paula to massage her lovely big breasts and she lifted her head to press her mouth over the bulging uncapped knob of his thick prick.

The sight of the beautiful girl holding Jock's cock while she lustily sucked his balls drove us wild and my hands left the keyboard to tear wildly at my trouser buttons so that I could release my huge erection that was threatening to burst through the crotch of my trousers. Sir Lionel was the first however to divest himself fully of his clothes and he sunk to his knees between Paula's legs and firmly removed the bottle that had been sliding in and out of her pussey and replaced it with his tongue as he licked and lapped at her juicy quim, his nose buried in her mossy mount.

'Now, Lionel, that's enough of your tongue − stick that thick prick up my cunt, there's a dear fellow,' cried Paula, her lips temporarily leaving the glistening shaft of Jock Gibson's meaty cock. 'I want it all. Oh, Lionel, please fuck me!'

As befitted a gentleman and a scholar, Sir Lionel raised his head to her titties and lapped at them in turn as the excited girl took hold of his throbbing tool and guided it herself, inserting the uncapped knob into the welcoming folds of her cunney. At the same time, Paula resumed sucking Jock's veiny staff, noisily slurping away as he fucked her mouth, his slippery shaft almost fully between her red lips, so that his knob must have been almost touching her tonsils.

She wriggled merrily as Lionel pumped his raging shaft in and out of her sodden cunney. Paula bucked and twisted, all the while urging the randy baronet to thrust deeper, deeper as she raised her elegant legs and wrapped them behind his broad shoulders. Cupped now in his palms, her tight little bum cheeks rotated savagely as he pushed in, pushed out and pushed back again, his balls slapping against her bottom.

John Walsh reached this lewd trio just seconds before me and Paula grasped his erect penis with her right hand leaving me to stand alongside Jock Gibson so that she could clasp her fourth cock, which was standing high against my belly, with her left hand. 'This is better than bridge,' declared John and we all chorused our agreement except for Paula, whose mouth was still engorged with Jock's huge cock, but she managed to nod her head slightly in agreement.

What a tableau greeted Bacon as he wheeled in a trolley of assorted sandwiches! There in front of his astonished eyes were Lady Paula naked on the Chesterfield being fucked by Sir Lionel as she fellated Jock Gibson whilst frigging John Walsh and myself with her hands.

The old valet stood transfixed as with a yell Jock shouted: 'Hoots! Here it comes!' as he ejaculated a veritable flood of spunk into her mouth. She swallowed as much as she could but the juice ran out over her lips and down her chin as with a grunt Lionel expelled his essence into her cunney, the white froth filling her love channel to trickle down her thighs. John and I were the next to spend which we did simultaneously, our fountains of spunk jetting upwards to rain down on Paula's large titties and we rubbed in the white love juice around her nipples as she herself shuddered with a most delightful series of climaxes.

We lay panting in an exhausted heap as Bacon cleared his throat and said: 'I have taken the liberty of running a bath, Sir, and perhaps you and your friends might like to allow Lady Platts-Lane to avail herself of the facilities.'

'What a splendid idea, Bacon,' I said and after Paula had finished in the bathroom we four men took showers before assembling back in the lounge where we refreshed ourselves with smoked salmon, caviare and champagne.

After we had quaffed our fill, Paula giggled and said: 'Larry, I have a confession to make to you.'

'Really, darling, and what might that be?' I asked.

'Well, I did not actually spend this afternoon quietly

41

discussing the formation of a new club with my friends Carolyn and Melanie,' she began.

'Ha, ha, ha,' laughed Sir Lionel. 'I'll wager a thousand pounds there is a man involved somewhere. Come on, Paula, don't be shy — who was the lucky fellow? Anyone I know? Jonathan Arkley, perhaps, or young Harry Price? Or is there some dashing new young man about town?'

'Oh, Lionel, I can never keep anything from your sharp brain. Well, if you must know, there were two boys involved,' admitted Paula. 'But I don't think I should really tell you exactly what went on.'

'You'll do much better if you make a clean breast of it,' suggested Jock Gibson firmly and John Walsh nodded his agreement.

'You won't be angry though, will you, Larry?' asked Paula anxiously. 'Promise me you won't be cross.'

'Of course I will, my sweet,' I reassured her, kissing her on the lips. 'After all, anything you did will pay me back for forgetting our arrangement tonight, though truth to tell I am well satisfied with the outcome so far this evening.'

Paula downed the rest of her champagne and said: 'Very well, then, I will tell all. I did take tea with Carolyn and Melanie and we did talk about the possibilities of starting up a new ladies club — but at five o'clock who should walk in but Carolyn's fiancé, young Antony Jammond, with his friend Fred Noolan. We chatted gaily to the boys about this and that but I noticed that poor Antony looked somewhat miserable and far from his usual bright, cheery self.

'"Is anything the matter, Antony?" I asked him. "Oh, don't worry about him, Paula," said Fred. "He is agitated over a personal matter and although I and several other friends have assured him there is no cause for concern, he cannot rid his mind of a foolish and unrewarding notion."

'"This sounds serious," said Carolyn. "Darling, do tell us what is worrying you. Perhaps we will be able to take the weight of whatever is troubling you off your mind."

'At first Antony was bashful but in the end he admitted what was causing him such anxiety — "It's the small size of my prick," he said. "I have noticed in the bath after cricket that all my friends are far better endowed than me. I am sure that Fred here, for example, can give the ladies far more pleasure with his huge chopper than I can with my relatively tiny little instrument."

'Melanie frowned and said: "It never ceases to amaze me that so many men are obsessed with the size of their pricks."

'"Yes, but we girls worry in the same silly way about the size of our titties," said Carolyn.

'"We're as bad as each other," I summed up, "for as everyone knows, it is quality not quantity that counts. As Jenny Everleigh puts it, what counts is not the size of the wave but the motion of the ocean!"

'"All very well," said Antony. "But ask any one hundred young men if they would like another three inches of cock, and if they answer honestly, you would find that the huge majority would reply in the affirmative."

'"I agree," said Carolyn. "And if you asked one hundred girls if they would like extra inches added to their busts, you'd get a similar result, I'll be bound."

'"Let's face it," added Antony, "we are not created equal. Carolyn would like a bigger bust and I would willingly give anything to be able to boast a nine-and-a-half-inch prick like Fred here."

'I gave Fred's crotch an admiring glance, for though I stoutly maintain that size is not all-important, I must admit that the sight of a big thick prick does cause my knickers to moisten! However, I turned my mind back to the problem of how best to show Antony and Carolyn the error of their ways.

'I decided that only a physical demonstration would show how misguided they were about this whole matter. So I asked if they would be prepared in a practical fashion to help me prove my point that size is immaterial so long as both partners are in receptive mood. They readily agreed and so, very sportingly, did Fred and Melanie who needed no persuasion to take my point of view but were eager to assist their misguided friends.

'To cut this story short, I began by instructing the two

43

men to leave the room, and to take off all their clothes upstairs in the main bedroom where we would shortly join them. After they left us, I explained to the other girls what they had to do and they laughed heartily when I explained my plan.

'We three also stripped naked but before we went upstairs, I borrowed three of Carolyn's silk scarves which I took up with me. When we entered the bedroom the two boys looked goggle-eyed at the three pretty naked girls and their shafts stiffened up nicely as we fondled their cocks and balls and let them play with our titties and cunnies. Then I blindfolded the two girls before guiding them over to a small table and telling them to bend over it. They obeyed, giggling, and the boys licked their lips at the sight of this pair of rounded bums thrust out towards them. It was time now to explain to Antony that he was to be blindfolded and I bound Melanie's scarf around his head until he assured me upon his word of honour that he could see nothing. At the same time I called for complete silence and for all conversation to cease.'

'What a splendid story, I can't think what you had in mind. I am sure we are about to hear of a most *recherché* happening,' said John Walsh enthusiastically offering Paula a fresh glass of ice-cold champagne.

'Hold on and all will be revealed,' laughed Paula, accepting the glass from the handsome literateur and *bon viveur*. 'Despite his blindfold, Antony's cock was still stiff as a poker as I grasped it and brought his sturdy shaft (which was admittedly only of average proportion) to the vale between Carolyn's well-rounded contours. "Listen, Antony," I said to him. "I am now placing the crown of your cock between the cheeks of this delightful girl's bum. Can you feel your knob sliding into her juicy grotto? Now gently thrust your shaft all the way in until your balls bang against her inner thighs whilst at the same time you take hold of her breasts in your hands and flick her titties up to stand hard and proud against your fingers. Let your prick throb its pleasure inside that juicy cunt but let it stay immobile until I tell you to begin fucking. And please

44

remember, everybody, if this experiment is to work there must be no talking."'

'I then turned to Fred Noolan and stretched out a hand to caress his huge prick which was at least two inches longer than Antony's instrument and whose girth was appreciably thicker. I rather fancied being fucked by Fred myself but my experiment had to take precedence. I inserted his cock into Melanie's cunney from behind and then said: "Very well, begin fucking but remember, not a word from anyone!"

'The lack of conversation did not inhibit in the slightest and the only sounds to be heard were the smacking of bellies to bottoms and the squelchy sound of pulsating pricks sliding juicily in and out of clinging cunnies. I frigged my own sopping pussey at the lascivious sight but I wanted a cock in my crack so I squeezed Fred's big ballsack and then Antony's smaller little bag to make them spend quicker. The touch of my soft fingers worked its magic and both boys squirted out copious emissions of love juice into their partners' pussies.

'Fred moved away and I was delighted to see that his glistening shaft was still semi-stiff. I took hold of Antony's hand and led him to the centre of the room where I took off his blindfold and at my bidding we all sat down as I began to question him. "Now, I know you will all promise to answer my questions truthfully," I said. "First, let me begin with Carolyn. Now, who do you think was fucking you just now? But before you answer, was the thick cock sliding in and out of your pussey big enough to satisfy you?"

' "I think it must have been Fred fucking me, Paula, for in answer to your last question, yes, indeed, the owner of the cock concerned can be justly proud of its length and girth. What a whopper! It stretched my cunney muscles delightfully."

'I said nothing but turned to Antony and said: "And which girl do you think had her love channel filled by your charger? I noticed that you had your hands around her breasts whilst you were pumping your spunk inside the lucky lady's pussey. Can they provide a clue?"

45

'Antony thought the matter over for a moment and said: "I really cannot be positive but as the girl concerned possessed ample bosoms and the most delightfully stalky nipples, I will plump for Melanie. Yes, I am sure that I was fucking her and not Carolyn."

'I bowed and said: "I rest my case. Both of you, Carolyn and Antony, wrongly judged the identity of your erstwhile partners and without any prompting from me you both stated how satisfied you were with the equipment a beneficent Creator has provided!"

' "A rock solid case," chimed in Fred. "I think they both owe you a debt of gratitude for neither should worry any longer about the intimate side of their future life together."

'To their credit, both Carolyn and Antony showered praise upon me but more than anything, I preferred to be rewarded by being fucked by Fred. The happy engaged couple left the room and left us to it. It was quite stimulating to see us both nude in the dress mirror and I pushed Fred down on the bed and kissed him passionately on the lips whilst my hand stole up and down his thick staff whilst his hands roamed freely all over my curvaceous body. Then shaking clear a fringe of hair from my face I leaned downwards to kiss the uncapped helmet of his cock and I opened my lips to take it in my mouth. I sucked slowly, tickling and working round the little "eye" on the top of the bulbous dome whilst Fred parted my unresisting thighs and inserted two fingers into my moist, longing cunt.

'I could feel a delicious sensation spread from my cunney to all over my body as he moved carefully across me. I was able to keep sucking his great cock as he managed to wriggle over and nuzzle my pussey lips so that we found ourselves in a perfect *soixante neuf*. He nipped lightly at my lips, running his tongue along the edge of my crack which fairly turned my insides to liquid. Oh, Fred was a marvellous artiste with his tongue and I tossed and turned as his wicked lapping in and out of my cunney brought me off to a spend. I sucked a little harder on his cockshaft and massaged his balls as I sucked away with relish. Soon I felt his balls tremble inside their sack and I judged that he was about to

46

spend. In a moment a stream of hot cream spurted into my mouth and his prick bucked as I held his knob between my teeth. Again, I enjoyed the supreme pleasure as I swallowed the copious rivulet of spunk that poured from Fred's magnificent cock. Then, as the last drops had been gathered up by my flickering tongue, I felt the spongy textured tool soften as I rolled my lips around it.

'But I mightily desired this magnificent cock in my cunney — and the question which had to be faced was whether Fred could build up another head of steam. I gently drew him over my body and directed his semi-stiff prick between my pussey lips. He was hardly fully ready for business but the instincts of nature triumphed as he helped shove his shaft inside my willing love channel. At first we lay motionless, billing and cooing with out lips, till I began a slight motion with my bum to which he eagerly responded. Ah, what ecstacy as I felt his thick prick swell inside my luscious sheath which received it so lovingly.

'How I enjoyed that delicious fuck! Fred opened the lips of my splendid cunney gently with his fingers and he cunningly frigged me with the mushroom helmet of his cock until I got so excited that I began thrashing around and shouted out: "Oh! Ah! Shove it in, Fred! Do push it in further, Fred darling! I must have it! Oh! Oh! Ah-h! Ah-h-re!" and I wantonly heaved my bottom upwards to each of his lustful thrusts.

'This was such a delightful engagement that I tried to keep Fred from spending for as long as possible. Once every last inch of his magnificent tool was inside me and our pubic hairs were mashed together, I closed my thighs, making this handsome young chap open his own legs and lie astride me with his cock sweetly trapped inside my cunt. Fred could not really move his shaft forwards or backwards as the muscles of my cunney were gripping his staff so tightly, but then I ground my hips round, massaging his shaft as it throbbed powerfully inside my juicy love-channel which was dribbling juices all down my thighs. He grasped my bum cheeks (something that I absolutely adore whilst being fucked) so I eased the pressure round his prick very slightly and he began to drive wildly in and out, fucking me at high speed which was most exciting.

'My pussey clamped down in a final burst of joy as his stiff, jerking prick gave a final throb before jetting out a torrent of hot cream deep inside me. I pushed my pussey up against him, burying his pulsating cock even deeper and let all that wonderful white froth bathe my inner walls as my whole body glowed with lust. Fred pumped away until his cock was milked of every last drain of juice and he slowed his thrusts to a halt. Panting heavily, he rolled off me and we lay gasping for breath as we gradually recovered our senses. What a magnificent cock! But even more important, as I gently reminded Antony, was that Fred was a passionate and considerate lover who would make any girl happy even if he had not had the good fortune to have been blessed with such a large instrument of pleasure. However, the thought did cross my mind that a big, big prick like Fred's did wet the appetite more than Antony's relatively puny little penis.

'We dressed ourselves after a refreshing warm bath and enjoyed our tea. Don't you all find how hungry one feels after a good fuck? We wolfed down sandwiches, cake and later toasted each other with a farewell glass of brandy.

'And that,' concluded Paula brightly, 'is how I spent this afternoon. It was a most energetic affair, but do you know, gentlemen, the recounting of these lewd happenings has made me terribly randy again. Perhaps I could prevail upon you, John, to fuck me as I have a great desire for it just now.'

Well, as readers of *The Oyster* will know, John Walsh does not have to be asked twice! In a trice the pair were thrashing around naked on the sofa and John was moving his hands around her gorgeous body with practised ease. He squeezed her firm breasts, rubbing the big dark nipples against his palms, making them rise up into little red stalks. He then began to kiss her entire body from her forehead downwards until he arrived at her open pussey and I could smell Paula's tangy feminine aroma as she guided the good-looking young critic's thick prick into her yearning wet cunney.

48

She wrapped her arms and legs around his well-built frame and urged him to make it 'hard and fast, John — let me feel every inch of your big tool.' 'As you wish, my love,' replied the literary cocksman politely as he slowly moved on top of her and Paula responded excitedly, opening her legs wide and clamping her feet round his back as he guided his throbbing shaft into her soaking little nookie. She took up the rhythm of his thrusts and I could see her legs shake and tremble and from my own encounters with Paula, I knew that she would soon be spending.

This erotic spectacle was too much for me to bear and I grabbed hold of my own swelling shaft and pulled my fist up and down, frigging it to its highest erection. 'Join in, Lawrence, join in!' cried Paula so I approached them, my cock in my hand as I knelt down to insert my knob into Paula's willing mouth. She grabbed hold of my cock and pulled three inches or so into her mouth, lashing my pole with her tongue as she sucked noisily away upon it.

Sir Lionel Trapes now approached us, his great aristocratic cock twitching uncontrollably in his hand, but just before Paula could grasp it he cried out: 'I'm spunking!' and he pumped out spurt after spurt of hot sticky cream over the entwined Paula and John, who, oblivious to their coating of jism were still panting and thrusting. The end was nigh, however, and I felt the sperm boiling up in my balls as with a gasp I shot a fierce jet of juice into Paula's mouth as John gave a powerful surging stroke and drenched Paula's eager cunney with a flood of frothy sperm as her hands grabbed his bum cheeks, pushing him deeper and deeper inside her until they collapsed, utterly exhausted, in a tangle of limbs on the cushions, and I must confess that the somewhat uncharitable thought flashed through my mind that I would have to instruct Bacon to sponge the sofa as soon as possible with Lady Gaffney's special stain remover as love juices can be the very devil to remove.

Well, Mr Editor, so ended the evening for me as Paula decided to spend the night with John Walsh and I was left to spend the night quite alone. As I wrote in the foreword to this missive, it certainly does pay to keep an accurate appointments diary, and I commend the diligent keeping of such records to all readers of *The Oyster*.

I am always, Sir, Your Obedient Servant,

(The Hon.) Lawrence Judd-Hughes
Dunton House
Albemarle Street
London, W
September, 1889

The Editor replies: Readers need not shed too many tears for Mr Judd-Hughes who must surely be one of the most famed cocksmen in Old London Town. We know for certain that in the last six weeks he has plugged the cunnies of Lady Emily Aldegonde, the ravishing young redheaded ingenue at the Drury Lane Theatre, Miss Beatrice Buxley and the lovely Lucy Lockette, the seventeen-year-old daughter of Lady Clare, after first having his way with her dear Mama the previous evening!

If these memories of past glories fail to mollify our correspondent let him remember the verse he himself penned in a previous issue of this magazine two years ago:

When wishes first enter a maiden's breast,
She longs by her lover to be caressed;
She longs for her lover to do the trick,
But in secret she longs for a taste of his prick!
Her cunney is itching from morning to night,
The stiff cock of her boy will yield her delight;
She longs to be fucked, and for that does deplore,
For what can a young maiden wish for more?
She'd like very well to be laid on the grass,
To have two ample bollocks sent bang 'gainst her arse,
If fever or sickness her spirits doth shock,
Why, we know what she needs, 'tis a stiff standing cock!

From Miss Deborah Davenport

Sir,

It is with pride that I pen this epistle to you for I believe that I can justly claim to be the first girl to be fucked by Mr Jeffrey Longbottom M.P. inside the portals of the House of Commons. Of course, I do not claim to be the first feminine recipient of Jeffrey Longbottom's cock in my cunney — his many conquests have been the subject of gossip in London Society for several years. However, I do claim the distinction of being the first to enjoy the pleasant sensation of lodging this clever politician's prick in my pussey during a Parliamentary debate, and at the suggestion of my old friend Sir Lionel Trapes (*see the previous letter from The Hon. Lawrence Judd-Hughes — Editor*) I now set down the circumstances of this historic coupling, which I trust your readers will enjoy as much as I delighted in partaking of this lewd experience.

I had met Jeffrey at a dinner party hosted by Doctor Le Baigue in aid of the Society For The Dissemination Of Useful Knowledge Amongst The Deserving Poor and I was pleased to find that I was sitting next to him during our meal. During the small talk that accompanies introductions, we discovered we had friends in common in Scotland and we had indeed met before (though we had not actually been introduced as such) at Colonel David Taylor's summer ball at his country seat just south of Glasgow. Anyhow, Jeffrey and I chatted about this and that and I asked him about the newspaper reports on rowdy scenes in Parliament — were they as bad as had been detailed in the newspapers?

'Not really, m'dear,' he replied. 'It is quite true that in the House of Commons we have nowadays occasional scenes of disorder which are not very creditable to us. And amongst the Radicals there appear to be a few ill-mannered individuals who seem unaware of their responsibility and who bring contempt upon the body of which they ought to be proud. But I am sure that this is by no means a new state of things and that in former times similar scenes occurred.

'After all, we live in a sensational age,' he continued. 'The popular papers take up a little *contretemps* and blow it up out of all proportion. So readers are told about scenes in the Commons and think that the country is going to the dogs. They forget, though, how smoothly and on the whole satisfactorily the Government of this world-wide Empire with its three hundred million subjects is being carried on.'

'That is good to hear, Mr Longbottom. However, I do hope that not all the business carried on is conducted in a terribly serious and formal way as I had planned to visit the House tomorrow as part of my studies for my entrance examinations to university.'

'Good heavens, you are not going to study Political Economy are you?' he gasped. 'Is a pretty young girl like you about to turn into one of these wild women who are demanding the vote?'

'I'm afraid that I am, but don't let's argue. After all, we won't convince each other of the correctness of our positions. And as I am sure that women will gain the vote in the end — for the tide of history cannot be turned back — there is little point in engaging in a debate.'

He laughed and said: 'By George, that's a fine way to win your points! I must use that trick in the House! But to reply to your original query, no, not all the business is conducted with great solemnity.

'It is a very curious thing but the House of Commons always seems to contain one amusing fellow. Mr Joseph Chamberlain told me only last week that there is always one wit in the House and when he dies or ceases to be elected, another springs up immediately to take his place.'

'Is he usually a Liberal or a Conservative?' I enquired.

'Oh, he could belong to either party for along with his predilection for buffoonery he has a hatred for which ever Government happens to be in office.'

Now it was just at this point, when the lobster bisque was being spooned into the tureens of Doctor Le Baigue's famous and indeed almost priceless seventeenth-century French china dinner service, that I felt a foot insinuate itself between my own and rub gently up and down my leg. Surely it could not be Jeffrey Longbottom for the Honourable Member had given no indication of amatory intent whilst he was speaking to me. I glared at the gentleman on my left but he was busily engaged in conversation with the lady on his own left flank . . .

The intruding foot continued its journey, rubbing sinuously against my leg, getting higher and higher and almost reaching my knee as Jeffrey concluded: 'Oh yes, m'dear, there will always be a place in the House for one chap who is a little cracked. He is there today, he was there fifty years ago and will doubtless be there fifty years hence.'

Yet still I could feel this mysterious foot which had insinuated itself between my feet and was now moving between my legs up to my knees. I glanced at Jeffrey and I could see that strange as it might be, it was indeed this handsome MP who, being a supple athlete, was moving his right leg in time to the movement I could feel underneath the table. I said nothing and he stopped caressing me with his foot until the ladies retired. I went straightaway to the powder room and when I emerged, he was standing in the hallway having taken his leave of Doctor Le Baigue and the other male guests in the dining room.

'I am bored by all the masculine talk in there,' he said lightly, pointing behind him. 'Why not join me upstairs for *tête a tête* coffee and liqueurs in Doctor Le Baigue's inner sanctum?'

'Will we not be missed?' I asked anxiously. 'Won't people start searching for us?'

'Unlikely, but even if they did, no guest would venture into Denis's little private room,' said Jeffrey cheerfully. 'It is so private that he fucks Kitty the chambermaid on Tuesday evenings and Betty Morgan the actress on Thursday afternoons here.'

'You are remarkably well-informed,' I said, trying to sound sophisticated rather than shocked at his frankness.

'Well, we are old friends and he often confides in me,' he replied simply, opening the door of the aforesaid room for me. Obviously, the rogue had prepared everything whilst I had been in the powder-room for there was a pot of steaming coffee on a gas burner and a fine selection of liqueurs arranged on a small table.

'Do you fuck, Debbie?' asked the rascally politician. 'I hope the question does not offend.'

I suppose I should have at least credited him with posing a question in a straightforward fashion but I was rather cross at the crudity of his approach. 'Yes, of course I do not refuse myself the pleasures of the flesh,' I replied. 'But I find your bluntness unappealing. Like the vast majority of women I prefer to be wooed.'

He begged my forgiveness and then insisted that it was my beauty that had captivated him; that the sight of my breasts bulging out of the admittedly low neckline of my evening gown had given him a huge hard-on which was still troubling him almost an hour later; and that he desperately needed to relieve his feelings.

I looked down and sure enough there was a meaty bulge in the area of his crotch. I leaned forward and stroked it and he groaned as I felt his staff pulse through the material of his black evening trousers. 'Oh, do take it out, Debbie, or I will spunk inside my drawers,' he whispered fiercely. I was now aroused and I could feel my pussey dampening as I unbuttoned his fly and drew out his cock. It was a fine specimen with a large ruby head and I took hold of the sturdy shaft and gave the ivory column a preliminary little tug. He smiled and placed his arms round me and I made not even a show of resistance as he raised my head upwards and closer to his own and our lips closed upon each other's and we melted away into a most arduous kiss.

54

I felt myself being borne back and we fell together, Jeffrey taking extreme care however that I would come to no harm in doing so. As our lips remained glued, he carefully unbuttoned my dress and somehow I managed to wriggle out of it. He pulled down my drawers and with a certain roughness that I did not find displeasing he thrust my legs apart, raising himself a little above me on one hand whilst with the other he pulled down his own clothing as the large knob of his cock pressed down upon my cunney lips.

'M'mm, that's nice,' I murmured as his knob continued to press into my wetness. For a moment our eyes locked together and then, with a heartfelt sigh, he inserted an inch or so of his thick prick and was full upon me. Our lips meshed and I wriggled my arse to obtain more of this meaty morsel. Jeffrey understood my need and clutching my naked bum cheeks, embedded his throbbing cock down to the root and in some magical way my cunney expanded to receive it . . .

'Would you enjoy a thick prick sliding in and out of your juicy love-channel, m'dear?' panted the randy rascal.

'A-h-r-e!'

I could not speak. I was filled by him. His big balls hung in their hairy sack beneath the bulge of my bum as his lips savaged my own. With a passionate jolt of his loins, he inserted the full length of his hard, smooth shaft inside my cunney. Then the rotter took out all but the very tip of his knob which made me beg for its immediate return! I know that some measure of modesty should be present at all times even in the first few moments of erotic bliss but I cried out unashamedly for his cock to be thrust back into my ever-dampening cunt.

We began to fuck in joyful unison, our bottoms heaving together as he worked his staff in and out of my luscious crack. 'Oh, what a delicious pussey you have,' he gasped. 'How tightly it clasps and sucks upon my cock! That's it, Debbie, work your arse! Ah, now not too much or I shall spunk before you are fully ready to receive my juice!'

55

Fortunately no-one entered the room during our joust, though in truth we were lost in that sensual world where fulfilment is all. Jeffrey's cock slewed in and out of my slit, pistoning back and forth and I gloried in each powerful stroke as my own juices sprinkled his balls. Cupped now upon his broad palms, the tight cheeks of my bum rotated savagely as his lusty tool continued to ram in and out of me at an increasing pace. I was now ready for his libation and I cried out: 'I'm almost there! Empty your balls, you big-cocked boy!' And with his face buried in my neck and his hot breath on my shoulder I could feel that he too was passing the point of no return. Though we both may have wanted it to last, we were very soon lost in the throes of orgasm and I felt my cunney awash with spunk as my pussey exploded around his throbbing cock. We were enveloped in the delight of a beautifully judged simultaneous climax as we collapsed in a rather undignified heap of limbs.

'That is a truly fine member you have there, Jeffrey,' I said, complimenting him upon his prowess, for I always believe in praising a good lover. Especially in London, I rarely fail to lavish affection when due, as unlike back home in Scotland, down South a hard man is good to find. Perhaps I lack the necessary information for a scientific appraisal, but my own empiric research shows that Scots possess thicker pricks than Englishmen – Jeffrey Longbottom, of course, is an exception to this rule.

We dressed hastily, for we did not exactly care to explain where we had been, and fortune was with us as we were not missed by the other guests. Jeffrey offered to escort me home but I explained that I had already booked a Prestoncrest carriage for the short journey to Brown's Hotel, Mayfair.

[*An interesting aside here – Prestoncrest Carriages was a coach (and later motor car) hire service used by a select band of people who knew that their drivers were sworn to secrecy about who was being transported to whatever address. Many illicit liaisons were consummated thanks to Prestoncrest vehicles. Amongst well-known men-about-town who were regular users of this semi-secret service were Sir Ronnie Dunn, Colonel Nettleton and the Society painter Ian Orpington — Editor*]

However, we arranged to take tea together the next day at the House of Commons and I hardly slept that night as I was so excited at the idea of being escorted round the grand Parliament Buildings.

Jeffrey had informed the attendant at the gate of the visitors' entrance that I was expected and a messenger was dispatched to find him. 'What constituency does Mr Longbottom represent?' I asked the gatekeeper.

'He represents Cockermouth in the Liberal interest,' said the liveried flunkey. How appropriate, I thought to myself, as Jeffrey's tall figure came into view.

'Hello, Debbie, how nice to see you,' he said as we shook hands. 'Look, if you're quick we could nip into the Lords and you could see Black Rod.'

'I saw enough of "White Rod" last night,' I said gaily.

'Ha, ha, yes indeed, and I trust you enjoyed the view. But as I am sure you know, the Black Rod to which I allude refers not to the colour of the King of Cameroon's cock but to the officer of the House of Lords and Order of the Garter whose job it is to summon the Commons at the Opening of Parliament.'

We didn't see Black Rod as a matter of fact but Jeffrey escorted me into the Distinguished Strangers Gallery of the Commons chamber where a debate on agricultural matters was taking place. The speaker, Mr Derek Tong, MP for West Kent, was droning on about the high incidence of poaching. He was railing about the pathetic pictures which are frequently painted of the game laws and the constant and pitiless persecution of the poor poacher.

'It is really quite laughable,' added Mr Tong, 'to all who know that during the last thirty years, poaching has been steadily followed as a "trade" by men who will not work even when work is plentiful and easily found. We can all sympathise with the occasional starving labourer whom some overzealous keeper has found with a couple of rabbits in his pocket which he had knocked over for his wife's pot;

but to bestow words of sympathy on the lazy scoundrels who shoot hares and net the partridge preserves must be left to the friends of humanity who become sentimental at the expense of sound old-fashioned common-sense.'

The debate continued and Jeffrey whispered to me how interesting it was to compare the colours of dress favoured by the honourable members. 'My friend Professor Trower says that to look our best, we should wear colours suited to our personalities.

'Strong, solid types like Arbuthnut Powell, the Under Secretary for Home Affairs, should dress conservatively in medium tones such as brown. Bright sparks like the Financial Secretary, Harry Price, look best in navy and in summer should forget any muted colours and go for striking shades.'

'An interesting theory,' I murmured over the drone of Mr Tong's voice. 'But not so interesting as that bulge between your legs, Jeffrey Longbottom.'

He grinned and sidled round behind me, looking around to check that there were no other visitors in the Gallery. When he was satisfied that the coast was clear he cheekily slid his hands under my dress and proceeded to pull down my drawers! I looked behind to see him unbutton his trousers and take out his swelling shaft, slipping the skin down to bare his purple-domed helmet. I licked my lips as I took his erect prick in my two hands and dropped down on my knees.

My hair tumbled over my face as I moistened my lips and let his knob slide into my mouth. I could feel his cock gliding in till it was at the back of my throat − I gulped and it slid down and down. He withdrew slowly and began to slide my lips slowly over his fat crown and then I was sliding my mouth faster and faster up and down that hot shaft. He bucked his cock in and out of my mouth and I could feel his balls slapping my chin. My climax was building quickly inside me as I felt Jeffrey's fingers in my hair and suddenly he grunted as his body went rigid and then his prick was bursting in my mouth and jet after jet of his thick salty spunk was hitting the back of my throat. I swallowed and swallowed, gulping down the tangy juice as I milked his cock of every drop of his jism.

Slowly his cock slid from my mouth and now it was my turn to gasp for air. But silently, the honourable member for Cockermouth laid me down on the padded bench and, throwing up my skirt, began to kiss and lick at my dampening pussey. He wiggled his tongue all around my crack. My senses reeled and I started moaning and panting as his tongue flicked against my clitty. I pulled his face tightly against my cunt as his lips slipped inside, his warm tongue prodding through my wet cleft to lead me to a little series of tingling peaks.

This was nice but I fancied a proper fuck, so I whispered to Jeffrey to lie on his back on the bench which he did with his noble cock waving like a flagpole, and then I sat astride him, pressing the lips of my aching slit down upon the glistening knob.

I spread my cunney lips apart and directed the tip of this glowing cock to the entrance as I slowly eased myself on top of him, spitting myself beautifully on his rigid rod. His hands slid round to clasp my bum as I wriggled around to work the hard staff as far up inside me as possible.

I bounced merrily away as I leaned down to Jeffrey and chuckled: 'Keep your cock up! Oooh! That's marvellous, you're giving my clitty a good rub as well!' Somehow we stayed silent as I worked my bum from side to side as Jeffrey jerked his hips up and down in rhythm to my own movements. But whilst I enjoy the so-called female superior position as a variant in one's pattern of fucking, it can be quite exhausting when your legs are in a cramped position as mine were on that bench. So I let the rhythm slow down as Jeffrey continued to thrust upwards to meet my own downward pushes.

Meanwhile, on the floor of the House, Mr Tong was still on his feet. 'From what is called "game",' he said sternly, 'the national commissariat derives an annual contribution of twenty-seven million pounds weight of wholesome and palatable food. Abundant evidence exists to show that sport wrongs no-one and benefits many. Those who rail against

59

all forms of sport should bear in mind that the pastimes of country gentlemen help thousands of the lower classes earn their daily bread.'

'Do you want to come now, Jeffrey?' I asked just as Mr Tong was building up to a rhetorical point. 'Is there anyone here who dares disagree?' he thundered.

'Yes! Yes! Yes!' growled Jeffrey, oblivious to everything except the boiling sperm that was building up in his balls.

Mr Tong looked up angrily at the Gallery where fortunately only my face could be seen over the rail. Luckily he could not see his fellow member's hands running freely across my breasts, tweaking the stiffly standing little nipples under the thin silk of my blouse. I smiled sweetly at Mr Tong who looked angrily at me but who, after a brief interlude, decided to return to his speech.

As he continued, with a fierce little groan Jeffrey worked his cock up inside me and commenced pumping his spunk in a copious emission until all was done and I lifted myself off the sodden shaft, still quite thick and long, as it dribbled its tribute in a snail's trail of white froth along his thigh. I had come several times and had also splashed Jeffrey's trousers with my spendings. 'Goodness me, I hope you are not needed to vote in a division,' I giggled softly.

'It's just as well that I'm not needed,' he murmured. 'It would take a far cleverer politician than me to explain away these spunky stains. Not even my friend Professor Trower could help me here!'

Coincidentally, the Speaker then called on the members to vote. 'All those in favour say "Aye"' he shouted. I joined in the chorus for though I am not and probably never will be a Parliamentarian, I think my conjoining with an honourable member entitles me to at least a footnote in Hansard!

A final word to feminine connoisseurs: Mr Longbottom's spunk is tangy enough but though plentiful, cannot compare in smoothness of flavour to that of the Duke of Hampstead or of the Laird of Midlothian.

I am concerned, though, Mr Editor, that my making love

in a chamber other than that of the bed will not upset the sensibilities of your many readers.

I am, Sir, Your humble servant,

Deborah Davenport
Castle Abroch
Loch Hayim
Scotland
October 1890

The Editor replies: It is to be hoped that Miss Davenport feels no worry about her enjoyment of this erotic encounter in the Mother of Parliaments. Again, let me use Lawrence Judd-Hughes' verse to illustrate my feelings upon the matter:

'Let maidens of a tim'rous mind
  Refuse what most they're wanting;
Since we for fucking were designed,
  We surely should be granting.
So when your lover feels your cunt,
  Do not be coy, nor grieve him;
But spread your thighs and heave your front,
  For fucking is like heaven.'

From Mr Henry

Sir,

I know it is the policy of your publication to print only letters which give the name of the writer. But I must beg your indulgence and pen this epistle under the cloak of anonymity for if my identity were to be established I would almost certainly lose my position as a private tutor.

I must explain that whilst the majority of my students are of a mature age and drawn from the very *crème de la crème* of our best families, very occasionally I am called upon to coach younger persons for school or university entrance examinations.

Perhaps I should add that I myself am the second son of a most respected clergyman whose parish is not a thousand miles from the parishes of St James and St George (*Mayfair* — Editor) and many parents entrust their sons and daughters to my unchaperoned care. Until last week, none of my students have distracted my attention from the work to be performed but as the old saw has it, there is always the first time . . .

Let me set the scene for you; picture if you will the study in my apartment near Baker Street. I await the arrival of Miss Tilly Diddlecombe and her younger twin sisters, Lottie and Eugenie. Tilly needed extra preparation for her final examinations at Bedford College where she is taking a degree in Modern Languages whilst her Papa, the Reverend Mark Diddlecombe, had informed me that he would be grateful if I could also assist Tilly's twin sisters who needed help with their French as they wished to gain proficiency in that tongue before setting off on a grand tour with Sir Timothy and Lady

Heather Shackleton, who as many of your readers know, take young people every summer on a cultural tour of the Continent.

It was last Thursday afternoon when I first set eyes upon my new pupils. My maidservant, Minnie, ushered the girls into my study and I must admit that my eyes fairly goggled as three of the most beautiful creatures I have ever seen walked demurely into my room. Tilly was twenty-one years old, somewhat tall and slender of build with shoulder-length reddish-brown hair that seemed to shine in the bright sunlight that was pouring through the bay windows.

As for Lottie and Eugenie, they were only just eighteen and both were as pretty, nay prettier than the girls whose faces adorn the boxes of expensive confectionery. They had come straight to their lesson from riding in Rotten Row with their boyfriends and were attired in white blouses which well accentuated their firm, well-shaped breasts, and tight riding trousers that moulded the contours of their tight little arses to perfection. Each had the face of an angel and a twinkle in their eyes as they apologised for not changing before coming to see me. I sat in my chair, fighting back an erection that was threatening to push my prick through the thin material of my flannels.

I passed round the syllabus for the first French lesson and caught sight of Tilly's tongue running over her raspberry-red lips, adding a glisten to her sensuous mouth which did nothing to bring down the bulge in my crotch. Then, still reeling, I spied Eugenie's hand slipping up Lottie's smooth thigh, rubbing sinuously up between her legs. Lottie moved her head back slowly, suppressing a sigh of delight whilst her sister's hand gyrated intricately above her crack.

'Excuse me one moment,' I said in a small choking voice. 'I will just check my own books before we start our French lesson.'

The girls giggled and Tilly said: 'Oh, Mr — — , never mind work for the moment. Perhaps you will appreciate another kind of French exercise at which my sisters and I are most proficient. Yes, I am certain you will prefer it to those boring old books. I know that we do, don't we, girls?'

'Very much so,' chorused the sisters as they joined Tilly in crowding round my chair. The elder girl smiled as she placed her soft hand on my raging hard-on that stood out like a sore thumb between my legs. She rubbed my crotch ever so gently as she turned her head to the twins and winked. I saw the outline of Lottie's nipples rigid under the straining cloth of her blouse as her twin sister caressed her breasts with one hand whilst she rubbed her own pussey with the other.

'You don't object if we call you Henry, do you, Sir?' cooed Eugenie.

I silently nodded my consent and then my attention was distracted as I felt my fly buttons being opened by Tilly's delicate hands and, in a trice, my eight-inch shaft was bared in her grasp. She slid her fingers up and down my truncheon, capping and uncapping my knob until she swooped down and sucked in at least half my eight-inch column into her saliva-filled mouth, lashing my cock with her tongue.

The twins now undressed each other and stood naked in front of me, their proud breasts jutting out defiantly as they moved their hands across to play with each other's auburn-haired pussies. Tilly realised that the sight of these two thrilling young bodies would speed the passage of sperm through my prick. So she alternated her lusty sucking with a nibble on the underside of my cock as she cupped my ballsack in her hand.

'As the eldest, I claim the right of having the first fuck with Henry,' said Tilly calmly. 'I think I would prefer to be taken from behind, if that is alright with you?'

I was only too happy to oblige as the sweet girl tore off her clothes with reckless abandon. Just the sight of her rosebud-tipped breasts was enough to cause some pre-come juice to dribble from the 'eye' of my helmet. Add to that the sight of her gorgeous, undulating bottom cheeks to those golden globes and you may well imagine the frenzy to be found in my loins. I raced over to the delightful girl who was now leaning over the mahogany table, waggling her bum in a most sensuous fashion. Holding my shaft in my hand, I entered her juicy cunney immediately and the warmth and smoothness of her velvet channel sent me into a delirium of delight. An added bonus was that there was a mirror on the wall facing us and it was an unbelievable stimulation to watch myself fucking this beautiful girl.

She squealed in ecstasy as I pumped in and out and she screamed out: 'Yes, yes, yes! More, more! Make me come!' It was easy to oblige and in seconds she was yelling and shaking as I brought her to a full climax as my own explosion burst through my staff, flooding her cunt with hot, creamy froth and she shuddered blissfully as she drained me of every last drop of love juice, as I pumped my fluids into her dark, secret warmth.

Now the twins clamoured for a taste of my cock and as I withdrew my still semi-stiff shaft from their sister's cunney, they handled my cock so cleverly that within a moment or two it was again as hard as steel. The twins dropped to their knees and took turns to suck my throbbing stalk as they played with themselves. This was too much to ask of any man — I just had to fuck them both and I gasped out the instruction that they should both lie down on the carpet with their legs spread wide to receive the gift of my throbbing truncheon.

Then I too dropped to the ground and rolled first onto Lottie, who returned my burning kiss with equal ardour as she took hold of my cock and guided it immediately between her pussey lips. After a few thrusts I leaned back and withdrew my glistening length. After all, how unfair it would be to leave Eugenie out in the cold. The sweet girl was rubbing her cunney in eager anticipation as I leaned over her and let her first kiss and gobble my knob for a few moments before I tit-fucked her, rubbing the crown of my cock on each of her nipples before finally sheathing my ecstatic column into her juicy cunt. I reached over to slide my hand between Lottie's legs and I massaged her pussey as I fucked Eugenie, ramming my cock in and out of her dripping cunney. Shrieks of delight left their breathless mouths and my own thrusts increased in tempo as a second spend fast approached. I flexed myself and with a hoarse cry poured out a luscious flood of creamy sperm into

Eugenie's cunney, which like her sister's was already awash with her own juices.

But, Mr Editor, now I was faced with a problem of how to satisfy poor old Lottie as both her sisters had reached the pinnacle of delight but my cock was in no state for a third game. Hard as the pretty girl tried, rubbing and sucking my limp penis produced no resultant erection.

I kissed the sweet girl passionately on the lips and laid her down on the carpet. Then I draped her long legs over my shoulders and dived down headfirst into her yearning love box. Her pungent pussey was already wet as I lovingly began to eat her, forcing my tongue deeper and deeper into the warm, juicy slit, sliding up and down the crack as I savoured her tangy aroma. Lottie gasped with joy as I probed between her cunney lips and thrust deep, finding her clitty which I rolled and sucked between my lips as she writhed around, rubbing herself off against my mouth. As I let the tip of my tongue dart in and out of her snatch she grabbed my head and pressed my face deep into her minge as she felt the first stirrings of a gigantic spend. Her juices dribbled like honey from her parted labia and her erect little clitty swelled even more as I flicked gently at it with the tip of my tongue. So I moved my hand up to my face and Lottie opened her legs even wider as I frigged her slippery clitty with my thumb. Her body was now jerking up and down which made the affair even more exciting as my face rubbed against her silky red bush. 'A-h-r-e!' she yelled as I worked my tongue around until my jaw ached, but I was rewarded by the lovely young girl achieving a tremendous orgasm, splashing my mouth and nose with her juices as her cunney spurted love juice all over the place until, as it subsided, she gently pushed my face away from her.

Well, the hour of tuition was nearly up and we dressed ourselves quickly, only just finishing in time before Minnie knocked on the door to announce the arrival of young Harry Barr whom I am tutoring for his entrance examinations to Oxford University.

The girls are due back tomorrow for a further French lesson and I will endeavour not to repeat last week's performance but actually instruct the delicious ladies in the French language. Whether I will be able to resist temptation is a matter upon which this pedagogue must ponder. Perhaps you, Mr Editor, with your vast experience of human behaviour, can advise me.

I, am, Sir, anxiously, ever Your Obedient Servant,

Henry 'X'
Marylebone,
London W.
April 1892

The Editor replies: I see no reason why you cannot teach these delightful girls the intricacies of irregular verbs whilst tickling their titties and playing with their cunnies. There is nothing wrong in combining work and pleasure. Are the girls cognisant of the important French words for pricks, pussies, etc?

I have taken the liberty of showing your letter to Mr Peter Stockman, the proud possessor of the biggest prick in London, and he assures me that his mighty penis is at your disposal should you need another stiff tool at your disposal during the next French lesson. Indeed, should you require a third, I understand Herr David Zwaig is in town and his continental cock is also available at no cost whatsoever should you require it. Both gentlemen may be contacted through my office.

From Miss Norma Radlett

Sir,

The merry month of May has always been known for its propitious influence over the voluptuous senses. It will give me the greatest of pleasure to share with your readers a little incident of such matter that occurred the day before yesterday when I went to visit my family's country seat in the heart of the Sussex countryside.

The house is a large enough residence, standing in spacious grounds of its own and surrounded by small fields of arable and pasture land, interspersed with numerous interesting copses through which run footpaths and shady walks where one is unlikely to meet anyone in a month of Sundays, even during the summer season.

Sheltered in many of the hollows in the hills you may find a Downland 'dewpond'. These are shallow depressions half-filled with water that may be seen on some of the highest hills of the Sussex range. The curious have often exclaimed on beholding these watering-pans which are well supplied with water yet with no apparent sign as to its source. In even a hot, dry season such as we have at present they very rarely fail the passing shepherd.

So when on a very warm afternoon I decided to cool myself by bathing naked in such a pond, I believed the chances of anyone else being in the area were slim. I had no idea that I was about to meet a rugged blond farmer's boy.

Jeremy was a real Adonis, tall and well-muscled but with the slender grace of a true athlete. I did not hear him approach as I splashed cool water round my dark pubic bush and at first I almost believed that he was part of a heat-induced fantasy. When I realised that he was in fact real, I jumped out of the pool and wrapped myself in a bath-towel that I had brought with me.

'I must apologise for disturbing you, Miss Norma,' he said with an engaging smile and not a hint of embarrassment.

'The fault was mine,' I said. 'But how on earth do you know my name?'

'We were introduced at Christmas at your parents' annual party for their tenants,' he replied. 'My father, Martin Lawbress, farms forty acres near Old Payning to the west of your fine mansion, and I had the pleasure of escorting you into the ballroom after dinner. But as I recall, you were suffering from a bad headache and you left the party before the dancing which was a disappointment, may I say, to me and every young man in the hall!'

I laughed. 'How kind of you to say so! I do remember you now, Jeremy Lawbress, and if my memory is correct you are attached to the purchasing office of Count Gewirtz of Galicia in London. I haven't seen the Count for some months now. Is he planning to visit England this year?'

'I doubt it as he has an invitation to spend the autumn in the United States with the President and he will probably go on to visit his Australian sheep farms,' said Jeremy.

'Really,' I said. 'He must be an extremely wealthy man. But is he a generous employer?'

'Oh yes, he is a surprisingly kind gentleman. When he was informed that I had suffered a severe bout of influenza, he telegraphed that I must take a long, fully paid leave at my parents' place in the country out of the poisonous London air, and that I should not return until I had fully recovered.'

Jeremy's handsome face attracted me and I invited the youthful lad to join me for an *al fresco* luncheon. As we sat there admiring the beauty of the surrounding countryside I could barely keep my mind on our conversation. I have not been involved with a man since last February and it was driving me insane to see this good-looking boy sitting across from me, the sun turning his blond hair into gold, and the smooth muscles rippling under his bronze skin when he took off his shirt to lie in the shimmering heat. I could feel my excitement growing and my love tunnel getting damper all the time.

It was hardly difficult to attract his interest. I shifted position, sitting so that my long legs were in full view and he was afforded just a hint of my pubic bush. This had the desired effect as Jeremy stopped in mid-sentence about the latest acquisition of Count Gewirtz, and had to swallow hard a couple of times before he could continue. His gaze travelled up and down the length of my legs and he now shifted somewhat uncomfortably as I noted with delight a bulge swelling up in his lap.

'It is so warm that I suggest we go in the water for a quick dip,' I suggested shamelessly, throwing off my towel and exposing my nude body to his glowing eyes. I stroked my large breasts suggestively before walking sinuously down to the water's edge and splashing my way in.

'Come on in, it's not cold at all,' I called out as Jeremy hesitated for a moment before shucking off his clothes and following me in. I noticed with satisfaction that he was blessed with a thick penis, already almost erect as he joined me in the pool, which was so small that we could scarcely help but bump into each other. As his hand brushed my hip I moved closer and stroked my fingers through the soft golden hairs on his chest. Jeremy took a deep breath and then decided to take what I was obviously offering to the lusty lad.

His strong arms wrapped themselves around me as our lips came together in a passionate kiss. I squeezed one of his tight little bum cheeks and brought his hips hard against mine. The throb of his rock-hard cock rubbing against my belly afforded me the greatest satisfaction and I was dying to find out what this huge sausage would feel like inside me . . .

Jeremy began by kissing my neck and shoulders and stroking my breasts until I was moaning and begging him to touch me. We climbed out of the pool and onto our piled-up clothes to continue our love-making. Jeremy sucked and

70

licked my nipples while his magic fingers played around my pussey, before moving down and letting his lips and tongue take over.

I adore having my pussey eaten and Jeremy's cunnilingal technique was quite superb, especially for a relatively inexperienced young fellow. He first knelt between my open legs and deftly parted my wet cunney lips with his fingers. Ah, how I shuddered as he smoothly massaged the inside of my pussey with his tongue, an arousing prelude rarely practised, alas, in this country although our continental cousins are adept at this arousing art. (Afterwards, Jeremy told me that Count Gewirtz himself had coached him in this valuable skill with ladies from Madame D'Arcy's salon in Brighton.) But now he moved from my inner lips to my clitty and began to suck on it very lightly as his hands moved up to my distended nipples which he rubbed in small, precise circles. I always find this produces a delicious sensation that courses throughout my body and already by now I was floating, my orgasm building up inexorably inside me. My love juices were flowing wildly as the tension grew and I could wait no longer to feel his bulging prick inside my raging love channel.

I let my right hand grasp his magnificent cock and, my God, was his penis big and stiff! There must have been at least nine good inches of it, hard as steel and panting with hot lust. Its thickness too was almost extraordinary and I could not fully wrap my hand around the throbbing shaft.

'What a whopper!' I exclaimed with undisguised admiration.

'Thank you, Miss Norma, it is very kind of you to so comment,' he replied modestly as I smoothed my fingers up and down this enormous pole.

At first he just teased me with this wonderful weapon, only inserting an inch at a time until I was crazy with lustful excitement. I rolled him onto his back and took his full length into my sopping crack, sliding up and down on my glistening charger as we thrust hard at each other, our cries of passion echoing around the empty hills until we spent together in a burst of ecstatic glory.

We lay together quietly for a time and then we went back to the pool to wash. To be certain that Jeremy's cock was really clean I began to lick and suck it until it was soon swollen up to full erection, standing stiffly up against his flat belly. This way and that I played with his cock in my mouth, now sucking deep, now licking only the very tip with the softest tongue of velvet. Jeremy sighed his delight, whispering to me how incredibly good my kisses felt and I was getting so turned on that I rubbed my nipples with one hand as I held his twitching tool in the other. Such high peaks of pleasure could not be long contained and all too soon his body tensed and he spurted a fountain of hot, creamy spunk down my throat. Not till his lovely cock had quite shrunk down did I withdraw my lips.

We returned to the bank to dry off and Jeremy finger-fucked me to another orgasm before we finished the afternoon with a final *soixante neuf*. It was time now to dress and return to our respective homes. Jeremy and I plan to spend further afternoons at the dewpond, but I shall have to journey to Doctor Nettleton's in Cocking for a jar of his famous cunney lotion for my poor pussey will need refreshing if Jeremy's mighty prick again batters her waiting portals.

I trust, Sir, that the loyal devotees of *The Oyster* will have enjoyed reading this true account of my unashamed lewdness as much as I have taken pleasure in recounting this tale.

Your humble (and happy) scribe,

Norma Radlett
Grove House
Lower Charlton
West Sussex
July, 1893

The Editor replies: Miss Radlett may be interested to hear of Professor Allendale's new idea for the easy insertion of big cocks into tight cunnies. He recommends the placing of the half skin of a peach, turned inside out upon the tip of the man's prick before he begins fucking.

Alternatively, a thorough sucking of the prick usually suffices. Lessons in this exquisite art may be obtained from Lady Margaret T —, Mrs Tessa P — and any of the inhabitants of a certain well-known house in Great Portland Street. Or again, readers may be safely recommended to purchase a bowl of cold cream from any reputable chemist.

From Mr Harry Wharton

Sir,

Undoubtedly one of the most remarkable evolutions of recent years has been that of the athletic girl. Against a hurricane of protest she has come surely and by deliberate intent into her own until, as the well-known (and aptly named) medical authority Professor Herbert Balls recently declared at a meeting of the Royal Society: 'the girl who has played games and entered into the spirit of games is not only the best made for any man who respects his comfort and happiness but is mentally and physically best suited to acquire a clearer and franker relationship with the opposite sex.'

My own observations upon this matter would seem to bear out the truth of the good doctor's remarks. For since taking up the sport of lawn tennis, my dear lady wife Helene has been a different woman who now is completely forthright about what she expects and enjoys in the bedroom. We have only been wed for six months and until now we have both been somewhat shy in telling each other what we most enjoy in the marriage bed.

Perhaps I should explain that as an Old Nottsgrovian (*See The Oyster Books 1 and 2, New English Library — Editor*) I have always been wary of being too forceful in *l'arte de faire l'amour*. It was rightly drummed into us by Doctor Simon White, our revered old headmaster, that no girl should ever be asked to do anything against her will. This excellent maxim still holds good, of course, but perhaps I have taken it a little too far and consequently been somewhat inhibited in even questioning whether we have experienced the full range of sexual delights of fucking and sucking and we have never been totally open in admitting our fantasies to each other.

Since Helene has taken up tennis, however, all this has changed. The first barrier we surmounted was the uninhibited use of language to stimulate our love-making. One night last week, after a particularly randy session, I was unable to restrain myself any longer and told my sweet wife how much I loved to fuck her dear little cunt. Rather than be angered by my use of strong language, Helene sighed that she loved my big strong cock above all and could not think of anything nicer in the whole wide world than being fucked by her powerful husband!

This lewd talk sent our blood boiling and during the next few days we hardly spoke of anything else. She would whisper about how she wanted to kiss and suck my hot, throbbing cock whilst I murmured my desire to lick and lap at her warm, wet cunney. Both of us would then hug and grab and grope before settling down into a delightful *soixante neuf*, my wife gobbling greedily on my helmet whilst I thrust my tongue in and out between her full cunney lips, nipping her erect little clitty playfully with my teeth, and you may well imagine that it took but a little while before my face was drenched in her juices whilst her mouth was filled with my tangy sperm which she swallowed with evident enjoyment.

Last Wednesday night came a real surprise of which I had not the slightest hint. We were lying naked on the bed and Helene was idly fondling my cock, rubbing my shaft up to peak erection and playfully capping and uncapping my knob as she pulled at my foreskin. Then suddenly she exclaimed: 'Harry, I must be totally honest and ask if you will take part in a very special little intimacy that I know will excite us both.'

'What exactly are you thinking of, my love?' I enquired, caressing the insides of her soft thighs.

'I want you to shave my pussey!' she whispered firmly in my ear.

Sir, I could hardly conceal my astonishment at this brazen

suggestion! At first I was speechless but then I thought to myself how interesting a shaved mound would be and Helene's wispy dark pubic bush would be easy enough to remove.

'Your wish is my command,' I said with a smile, and within a few minutes I had organised a bowl of hot water, scissors, shaving cream and a safety razor. First, I just clipped her bush but then I spread the cream all over her pubic hair and carefully proceeded to shave the lot away! I shaved around her thick, red outer cunney lips until all that could be seen, clear and true, was her bald pussey. I handed Helene a small mirror and she squealed with delight as she took a good look.

After cleaning her up with a warm washcloth I rubbed a light oil over her now even more voluptuous cunt. By this time we were both feeling extremely randy and my cock stood up like a flagpole as Helene lay down and spread her legs invitingly. I needed no further encouragement and went down on her without pausing. I chewed and lapped at her cunney lips and let my tongue dart between them to find her erect little clitty. After rhythmically circling it with the tip of my tongue, I nibbled and sucked on the dear morsel and indeed she tasted even better than before. She spent passionately over my face before I withdrew and substituted my knob in place of my lips. Helene eagerly thrust up her hips as my cock slid into her sopping crack. She threw her legs over my back and heaved up and down in time with me as we commenced a most excellent fuck. Despite her own libations, her cunt was exquisitely tight, holding me in the sweetest vice imaginable, so much so in fact that I could feel my foreskin being drawn backwards and forwards with every shove.

But her juices were now flowing so freely, oiling her cunney walls so well that my further thrusts were made easier as my trusty tool buried itself within the luscious folds of her shaven slit.

'Harry, Harry!' she yelled. 'Now, my dear husband, fuck me hard! Push in, push in, there's a love. Oooh! How marvellous, how gorgeous, how you make me spend!'

I made one last lunge forward, my balls banging against her bum cheeks as with a hoarse cry of triumph I shot a stream of hot spunk into her pulsating pussey. I wriggled my shaft around inside her as the sperm continued to gush out of my prick in great jets as we writhed around together, enjoying this great fuck to the full.

On Sunday night we discovered a further bedroom delight and I do not believe it to be merely coincidental that it arose after Helene had taken part in a hard-hitting game of tennis with Mrs Fitzcockie, the Northern Area champion.

Let me note here that neither of us were ignorant of the practice of masturbation but we had not imagined it to be part of our sexual relationship. Last Sunday evening proved how wrong we were!

Often, before and during a fuck, I would bring Helene to orgasm by playing with her clitty. Occasionally, I would bring her hand to play with her pussey but before now she was reluctant to do so. On this night, however, I simply asked her to finger-fuck herself and she took off as one obsessed! Whilst I was inserting my cock in her cunney from behind as she bent over the bed, she reached down and grabbed her clitty and manipulated it superbly. She soon reached a tremendous orgasm moments before I spunked my stream of juice into her cunt from between her bottom cheeks.

Since then she has been doing this whenever I ask her — and occasionally even when I don't — and she even finger-fucked herself in our carriage on the way to Sir Andrew Stuck's literary soirée in Bloomsbury the other evening.

Helene is a most stunning creature and it is a beautiful sight to see her writhing in ecstasy as she masturbates, her shaved pussey arching upwards as she approached her spend, her head thrust back and her tits straining against the thin material of a summer blouse.

Indeed, yesterday afternoon Mr Colin Ramsay, the well-known photographer, came round to our house to take some portraits of Helene in the nude and she put on a special performance for the great man; and there is one shot (for

Mr Ramsay was so excited that he worked all night to be able to show us some sample proofs early this morning) of Helene, one hand caressing her nipples and the other fingering her cunney, that deserves publication in your esteemed journal.

I must add that after Mr Ramsay left this morning Helene insisted that I join in the fun and toss myself off in front of her, an idea that had indeed crossed my mind. At first I was hesitant, not having wanked in front of anyone since our circle jerks in the third form at Nottsgrove. However, after swallowing a large whisky and soda, I pulled off my clothes and took my penis in my hand. My initial shyness prevented me from really letting go but then I gradually got into the swing of things and my hand sped faster and faster along my shaft until with a gasp I shot a stream of semen all over Helene's waiting titties and she rubbed in the white juice over her stalky strawberry-coloured nips.

Incidentally, my wife's tennis has much improved too and tomorrow afternoon she is playing in the London and Middlesex Championships at Hendon. Those knowledgeable in the game confidently expect her to reach the final rounds and if Helene plants her drives and volleys with as much grace and enthusiasm as she now shows in her fucking, I do believe that I will soon be the proud husband of an international player. So I have a great deal of which to be thankful to the game of lawn-tennis, which is why I have today donated two thousand pounds to the organisers of women's tennis so that more young ladies will be encouraged to take up this most edifying of all sports.

I believe that all patriotic men should follow my example for in conclusion I quote again from the lecture given by Professor Balls: 'The husband of an athletic girl may find his friends wondering why he does not sigh for the "foolish little thing" of other days. But in place of the fragile young flower, prone to swoon at every turn, we now have a growing number of well-built young women of amazing cheerfulness and vigour with a grip on life and upon themselves.' And indeed, if I may be so permitted to add, upon their husbands' cocks!

Yours faithfully,

Harry S. Wharton
Watford Lodge
Rondunn Road
Hampstead
London, N.W.
August, 1894

The Editor replies: My sincere congratulations to the gallant gentleman and his lady wife on discovering that all forms of fucking tend towards achieving the acme of felicity.

Captain John Gibson of Edinburgh, who happened to be in my office when your letter arrived, suggests there is a further avenue which you may care to follow, best expressed in the following verse:

There was a young lady of Glasgow,
And fondly her lover did ask: 'Oh,
  Pray allow me a fuck,
  But she said: 'No, my duck,
Though you may, if you please, up my bum go!'

From Miss Fiona Bunter-Dunne

Sir,

I am happy to share with readers of *The Oyster* the ecstatic experiences of some fine fucking I was recently privileged to enjoy on a railway journey to Bonnie Scotland.

As a demure (sic) young girl of just nineteen, normally I would have been chaperoned on the night sleeper to Edinburgh. But my mother's companion, Miss Harrow, had turned her ankle quite badly that very morning, after tripping up over Rex, our pet corgi, so to my great joy it was decided that I could travel alone as Cripps the butler would escort me to Kings Cross Station and I would be met at Waverley, Edinburgh by Colonel McGraw's personal carriage.

I was travelling to Edinburgh to attend the coming-out ball of one of my oldest friends, Susey McGraw, in whose company I spent not only my schooldays at St Hilda's Academy in South Devon but also a year at Fraulein Metternich's Finishing School For Young Ladies in Zurich, Switzerland. Susey and I both lost our virginities during the first term at Fraulein Metternich's to the same handsome young mountaineer, Konrad Kochanski, but that is another story which, Mr Editor, I will relate at a later time if you so desire.

Be that as it may, when I boarded the train five minutes before we were due to depart, the first class lounge was almost empty, and by half past eleven all the other passengers had retired except for two young men who invited me over to their table for a nightcap. This sounds terribly forward but I must hasten to add that Kevin Durie (of the

80

Argyll Duries) was known to most of the best families in London and had been a guest only the previous month at one of my mother's musical evenings where we had been introduced. The older of the two — previously unknown to me — was none other than that infamous man about town Sir Andrew Stuck, whose reputation was of course known to me although I had not had the pleasure of being introduced to the handsome young baronet before this unexpected meeting.

'I did enjoy your mother's concert, Miss Bunter-Dunne,' said Kevin politely. 'I am particularly fond of Mendelsohn's string Octet which I thought the little orchestra played with great brio.'

'Yes, it is a fine piece of music,' I agreed. 'The piece has astonishing instrumental and contrapuntal skill that serves an original conception of delightful freshness. It is quite extraordinary to think that Mendelssohn was only sixteen years old when he composed it.

'Are you fond of music, Sir Andrew?' I asked.

'Not overmuch, to be honest,' he grinned. 'I prefer the theatre to the concert hall and a rousing chorus of a Gilbert and Sullivan show to the boring dirges of many of the so-called classical composers.'

'Not only are you a Sassenach but you are also a barbarian,' grinned Kevin, but we chatted amicably enough, polishing off an alarming proportion of the bottle of malt whisky Kevin had brought with him to while away the journey.

Then the door opened and who should come through but Clare Corisande, another alumni of Fraulein Metternich's establishment (and who had also been deprived of her maidenhood by Konrad Kochanski, by the by) and who was also bound for Edinburgh and Susey McGraw's dance. Her Aunt Maud, who was accompanying her, was fast asleep in the lounge. She knew Sir Andrew very well and I was pleased to introduce her to Mr Durie. In honour of this pretty girl, whose blonde tresses I had much admired, we finished Kevin's bottle and then prepared to make our way to the sleeping compartments.

But as we rose, Sir Andrew said: 'Tell me, ladies, are either of you familiar with Scottish dress?'

'Not really,' said Clare. 'Indeed, this will be the first time I have been North of the Border.'

'Well, they have some curious customs in Scotland,' grinned Sir Andrew. 'For instance, let me show you a photograph of Kevin here in his kilt at Lord Bourne's ball.'

Clare and I looked at the photograph of Kevin in what appeared to be a tartan petticoat which left his knees naked to the elements.

'Did you waltz in your kilt?' asked Clare mischievously.

'Aye, I did, right enough,' said Kevin. 'And why not?'

'Oh it is just that I would have thought that the whirling motion of dancing would have caused your kilt to fly up and expose your . . . ' and she stopped suddenly and giggled.

'Arse, you were going to say, Clare,' chipped in Sir Andrew gaily. 'Well, what would have been the harm in that? Girls like to get a glimpse at a man's firm bum cheeks sometimes.'

'Andrew, hold your tongue,' scolded Kevin, colouring as we looked again at his photograph.

'I have a far better one taken from the front,' leered the randy baronet, taking another photograph out of his wallet.

'Don't you dare!' panted Kevin, trying without success to grab the offending picture, but Sir Andrew laughed and passed it across to me. My eyes widened as I looked at it for there was Kevin, holding up his kilt to show that nothing was worn underneath that garment. His prick looked of a fair proportion, a thought that crossed Clare's mind as she told me afterwards, and we both noticed how Kevin's heavy balls hung low in their hairy sack.

'Kevin,' said Andrew. 'I do not believe that the girls think the sight of your Caledonian cock is more beautiful than the view of your bottom.'

'Well, that proves that our education has not been neglected,' said Clare boldly. 'For as the catechism puts it: "What is the chief end of man?"'

'My dear girls, we are all quite private here as the guard has gone to his compartment. Would this not be a fine opportunity for you to view the genuine article? Come on, Kevin, be a sport and show the girls your prick in the flesh,' said Sir Andrew. 'Meanwhile, you must excuse me for a minute whilst I answer a call of nature.'

Kevin blushed but I said: 'Now then, don't be shy. Both Clare and I are familiar with the sight of a naked prick. We will give you our honest judgement upon the dimensions and general look of your staff of life.'

'If you insist, then,' he said, unbuttoning his fly and baring his erect cock. 'I am always ready to please the ladies.'

Clare and I inspected his tool and we told him fairly and squarely that it was as big as he had any reason to expect and was well-fitted for all but the most cavernous cunt.

'I would be more than happy to entertain this cock in my cunney,' said Clare, moistening her lips with her tongue.

'So would I,' I agreed and I took hold of Kevin's rock-hard shaft and gave it an encouraging little rub. A few moments later the three of us were in his compartment, all quite naked and kissing and cuddling up together. I found myself on my back with Clare lying on top of me, our tummies and breasts pressed together with her legs stretched out between mine. Kevin moved between her legs and, after he had pulled her up to him, pushed his prick deep into her bum-hole. As he fucked her wrinkled little rosette she moaned and sucked upon my own rosy titties and when he spunked into her arse she almost achieved a climax herself as she grabbed my hands and held them very hard.

Clare then pulled one leg over mine and pushed her thigh up against my cunney. We were both wet with love juice as she began rubbing her lithe body up against me. Kevin moved his head towards my face and we kissed, our tongues inside each other's mouths as Clare continued to rub sensuously against me. He now climbed up on top of us and placed his twitching tool against my lips. I opened my lips to suck in his helmet and I lashed the succulent shaft with my tongue before taking in another three inches of his delicious cock in my mouth.

Meanwhile Clare was now kissing my erect little titties and

83

I could see the shadowy figure of Sir Andrew Stuck in the background, undressing as fast as he could. In a trice, the randy baronet had his cock in his hand and was sliding in beside Clare, guiding his mighty rod towards my waiting cunney lips, which opened as if by magic to enclasp the crown of his thick tool.

All three were now fucking me in perfect rhythm and it was the most exciting sensation I have ever experienced. I came simultaneously both with Sir Andrew who spurted a copious emission of spunk splashing against the walls of my juicy cunt, and Kevin who filled my mouth with his frothy white jism so wonderfully well that I could not gulp it all down and some of the juice ran down my chin.

After a short intermission we paired off and I lay down with Kevin as I had not yet had the pleasure of having his cock in my cunney. We embraced in a kiss of blazing ardour and then his tongue moved downwards from my mouth, circling one nipple and then the other as they hardened under his tongue. I purred with pleasure as I ran my fingers down the length of his shaft, and then delved underneath to tickle his unusually heavy balls.

He must have read my mind for he said softly: 'They're overflowing with spunk and it's all for you, Fiona,' as he slipped his arm around my waist and pulled my bum up so that my dripping cunney lips were brushing against the tip of his knob. For a few moments he continued to tease my sopping crack as he rubbed his knob all along my slit, but then at last he slid the bulbous mushroom head into my welcoming cunt and began fucking me with long, gentle thrusts.

I could feel his lovely staff getting even larger inside my cunney and he groaned, reaching up to tweak my titties with one hand and fondle my clitty with the other. My juices were now simply seeping out of me as he flicked that little button backwards and forwards as he continued to move his shaft slowly in and out of my pulsating pussey. His hips were thrusting that hard rod further and further up me and the walls of my love channel were opening and closing around

84

it. And then whoosh! with a great shudder he creamed my cunt with a huge flow of hot sperm.

After that I reckoned he would need some time to recover, but as he removed his sticky shaft from my pussey I could see that it was still stiff and would need only a little help to regain all its former glory. I slid down his chest to crouch over his knees, leaving a trail of love juice all the way down to his belly. Whilst his cock was still wet I clamped my lips round it and tasted our combined juices. They were quite deliciously tangy and I could not resist a lusty suck of Kevin's big balls before tonguing his shaft up to its full height and hardness.

I lay back to receive a second shafting from this majestic prick, but as he inserted his cock as far in as possible so that our pubic hairs matted together, I decided to change positions. Still holding his staff firmly inside me by contracting my cunney muscles, I rolled over on top of him and sat astride his broad chest to ride him in what turned out to be a magnificent St George. I bounced happily up and down, pivoting gracefully on this throbbing column as we spent almost together, our juices mingling in a further flood of mutual jism.

As we lay recovering from our exertions, I glanced over to see that Sir Andrew was being given the full treatment by his delightful partner. He was lying flat on his back whilst the gorgeous girl was holding his erect prick in her hands. She wet her lips and knelt between his long, muscular legs and then took the finely formed crown of his cock between her lips, clamping them around his not inconsiderable shaft, her blonde tresses spreading along his thighs as he jerked his hips upwards to stuff as much of his shaft as he could inside her soft mouth.

But when he tried to establish a rhythm, she lifted her head and giggled. 'No, Andrew, I would rather have your big cock inside me, if you please,' she said, and straddling his body she pushed herself down upon his sturdy truncheon, squeezing his thighs with her knees and riding him like an American rodeo rider, pushing him harder and harder until he spent with a husky groan.

At once, Clare rolled off and propped herself on one elbow, watching Sir Andrew's face as she traced delicate patterns along his limp prick. 'Are you all done so soon?' she teased. 'Let me see if there is any more spunk that I can milk from your lovely cock.' The handsome baronet sighed and said: 'I fear that what you see is all you will get.'

'I think you are capable of better things,' said Clare, and before Sir Andrew could reply she began licking the perspiration from his body — first his chest, then along his arms and legs. Her hands cupped his bum cheeks, probing and massaging and lo and behold his prick began to stir again and with a smug smile Clare said: 'Just one little suck should do the trick.'

She rolled his stiffening white column between the palms of her hands and sucked his helmet into her mouth. Her prognosis was absolutely accurate for it took only a few seconds before she withdrew her lips a second time from his now rock-hard prick and smiling smugly, she knelt on all fours in front of him, thrusting her firm white buttocks into his face. 'Now give me a firm pressing of juice up my bum!'

Nothing loath, Sir Andrew scrambled up to mount her, his left hand prising open a channel between the cheeks of her splendid arse, the other holding his massive blue-veined tool that had risen rigid from its nest of dark curly hair. He forced his knob to the rim of her wrinkled little brown bum-hole and Clare cried out at first as he slowly forced his huge knob inside after wetting it with some spittle. But then her sphincter muscle gradually relaxed as he entered the tightened orifice and she told him to sink in all of his shaft up to the hilt.

Sir Andrew leaned forward to fondle her breasts, his eyes bright with excitement as he pounded his shining, slippery shaft into her lithe young body. His prick rose in and out of its narrow sheath, plunging in and out of the now widened rim, pumping and sucking like the thrust of a steam engine.

'Ah, Clare, what an arse, what warmth, what tightness!' groaned the lucky young rascal, patting her flanks and savouring no doubt the plump rondeurs of her bottom cheeks against his belly. A gentle movement of Clare's hips sufficed to show the pleasure she was evidently sustaining.

'Do not move your cock for a moment! Oh, Andrew Stuck, fuck my bum, you big-cocked boy!'

And with those lewd words, the pretty blonde reached back to spread her cheeks even further, jerking her delicious bum to and fro until, with a tremendous shout which I feared would wake the sleeping passengers, Sir Andrew shot a jet of frothy sperm inside her as they spent together in perfect accord.

He withdrew his still semi-hard prick with an audible little plop and we all lay together in a sweaty tangle of arms and legs.

I have always wondered, Mr Editor, why the male of the species is known as the stronger sex for both Clare and I were ready and willing to continue this sensuous joust, but both Kevin and Sir Andrew were now deep in the arms of Morpheus and we girls were forced to play with each other for the next hour or so — not that I minded too much, for Clare managed to bring me to a truly superb spend. I just about have enough time left to tell you about how she did it . . .

She began by licking her finger and placing it at the base of my throat. And then slowly, very slowly she traced a line down the middle of my body. She kept licking her finger so that it was always wet as it slid down my body, between my breasts, over my belly and down into the silky dark curls of my pussey hair. Then she insinuated the other between us and manipulated my firm breasts, tweaking my rosy nipples up to a peak of hardness and I gasped and twisted for the caress was even more enervating than I had judged and my aroused globes seemed to swell to her touch.

The tips of our tongues met and then we were exchanging the most burning, the most devouring of kisses as my own arms wrapped themselves around the sweet girl. I gasped again as Clare carefully slid her knuckles around my oily cunney lips and at this first ardent rubbing of my pussey I was on my way to Elysium. My legs parted, enabling her to slip full length upon me. Withdrawing her urging finger, her furry blonde mound now nestled moistly against my own. My whole body tingled as I felt the rubbing of our cunt lips, the tingling merging of our pubic hair as, coiling her arms under my knees and raising and thrusting my legs back, she caused our cunnies to meet and rub fully together. I clasped her shoulders as our bottoms squirmed in mutual delight. Very soon, a violent shuddering racked my body as I achieved an enormous spend and my cunney spattered out its juices all over Clare's blonde bush.

With a sigh, the gorgeous girl rolled off me and I kissed her sweet lips saying that I would now ensure that she too achieved the delight that I had just had the pleasure of experiencing.

How could I best have my way with the beautiful blonde girl who languidly stretched naked before me, purring like a kitten, her legs wide open and her hand playing around the silky hairs of her golden pubic bush?

Without hesitation I rolled on top of her and licked her titties up to a fine state of hardness, letting my eyes feast on her delicious pussey. The blonde hairs were silky and the lips looked oily with the excitement of our previous encounter. Oh, how she wriggled and writhed as I worked my tongue first into the whorl of her navel and then my lips slithered down to her hairy mound until they were directly over her eager quim and I could inhale the unique feminine aroma from the rich cunney juices which were already flowing freely from her. I parted her thighs to ease my head down into a comfortable position and then plunged my pointed tongue back and forth inside her pussey. Clare squirmed under my ministrations, pressing her mound up against my nose and almost threatening to choke me with her hairy muff.

'Oh, Fiona darling, don't stop now!' she pleaded as I paused for breath.

She need not have been concerned as I had no intention of ceasing to suck that delicious cunt. My tongue slid through her smooth passageway and outlined the mound of her erect little clitty which rose up to greet me. I licked and lapped all around it, sending Clare into a delirium of

88

delight as her legs waved this way and that as my tongue continued remorselessly to slurp around it. Then I took the pulsating morsel in my mouth, rolling my tongue around it and nipping it ever so gently with my teeth. She squealed with joy as I continued to work my tongue until she heaved violently, arched her back and then came in a fierce spurting. My hand slipped under her comely bottom and as her love juice flowed out, I worked my forefinger in and out of her bum in a most exciting way.

I continued to suck her cunney until her orgasm finally faded and we lay happily together as the last drains of our juices were released, oiling our thighs as we too now fell into a deep welcoming sleep.

By the time we reached York the boys had woken up again although Sir Andrew was still a little groggy. However, I sucked his balls which had the desired effect and we formed a nice little fucking chain that lasted almost until we passed Tyneside. I lay on my tummy, thrusting my bum cheeks out towards Kevin who fucked my pussey from behind as I gobbled Sir Andrew's thick prick. Meanwhile, Kevin had his hand working in and out of Clare's cunney as she kissed Sir Andrew, whose hands roved along her bosom, his hands squeezing and caressing her jutting young breasts. Clare and I changed over and after she rummaged in her travelling bag for a 'ladies travelling companion', or dildo as the common vernacular has it, we were able to vary our positions.

Perhaps my particular favourite 'wholesome foursome' was fucking Clare's lovely bottom with the dildo as she sucked away on Kevin's smooth shaft whilst the dear lad was lapping at my pussey. At the same time I used my other hand to toss off Sir Andrew as he tongued Clare's cunney in rhythm with her bottom fuck afforded by my thrusting of the dildo (which was bound in soft leather) in and out of her arse.

As you may imagine, we were all quite exhausted by the time we reached Edinburgh, but it did not stop us enjoying a grand holiday in the Athens of the North. Susey McGraw's dance was a great success and she has just sent me a photograph from the Scottish Tatler which shows me in conversation with her cousin, Jack Webster of Aberdeen, a most good-looking young man whose cock was to enter my love channel some three hours after the photograph in question was taken!

Alas, *tempus fugit*, Mr Editor, and I must now close for I am already late for my appointment with Monsieur Josef, the new French hairdresser in Bond Street much favoured by Society since Princess Alexandra became a regular patron earlier this year.

However, I must not forget to add a footnote from dear Clare — she is presently spending the summer in Italy with her Papa and Mama at Lord Horn's villa and would be grateful to hear from any gentleman of good family between twenty and thirty-five who might be visiting that country from now until September. She may be contacted by telephone (Florence 1189) or by post at Via Cavour 69, Florence, Italy.

Yours in haste,

Fiona Bunter-Dunne
21 Belgrave Square
London S.W.
June, 1894

The Editor replies: A splendid letter, Fiona, and reading your adventure sent my pego standing stiffly to attention. Fortunately, Miss Reddie, my faithful secretary was on hand to suck me off or I would have been forced to indulge in a five knuckle shuffle.

Do accept, with my compliments, the gift of a magnum of champagne and feel free to come round to my office at any time. And do give the young rogue Sir Andrew Stuck my kindest regards when next you see that randy baronet.

From Mr Clive Kinison-Jones

Sir,

After our final examinations at Trinity College, Cambridge this summer, members of the Epicurean Society at this august seat of scholarship decided to hold a ball — and I was lucky enough to find a girl who was prepared to take this invitation literally!

There must have been some forty of us crammed into the supper rooms at Mr Burbeck's famous hotel (and there being only ten or so girls from the neighbouring college for schoolteachers, I was hardly optimistic about the chance of a kiss let alone a fuck). Anyway, our senior tutor Dr Tagholm began the proceedings with a spirited rendition of an old Sussex drinking ditty sung at harvest suppers in that rustic county. It goes like this:

'The miller's old dog
Lay on the mill floor,
And Bango was his name, O!
B-A and N-G-O
And Bango was his name, O!'

Then he instructed us on how the company should join in. Now the method of singing this song was as follows: the leader would sing the verse, repeating the fourth line thrice and then turning to his right-hand neighbour, would say 'B', the next man would say 'A', the third 'N' the fourth 'G' and the fifth 'O' whereupon we all had to roar out the chorus — but if any singer missed his proper letter he had to drink a glass of champagne — hardly an onerous forfeit!

Well, an inexperienced group such as ours made quite a few mistakes and within a short space of time we were all very merry indeed! To cut a long story short, after half an hour or so I got up and answered a call of nature. As I washed my hands, however, I noticed in the mirror that the door was open and leaning against the wall in the hallway was a perky little blonde girl whom I had noticed sitting with her friends in front of me. I smiled at her as I came out and we exchanged some small talk and later our forenames.

'I was looking for the ladies' room but I fear that I have been misdirected,' she said, a delicious dimple appearing on her right cheek as she smiled.

'It is just down here on the left,' I said, motioning the way with my arm. 'I will wait here and escort you back when you have finished.'

'Thank you, Clive, how nice of you,' she said and, well, again, to be brief, when she returned we agreed that it was too noisy a party for our liking and she accepted my suggestion to see my rooms which were only over the way in my college.

It was easy to smuggle her past the doorkeeper and once in my room Lizzie herself closed the door and locked it. As soon as I turned round this little vixen was all over me. 'Ah, you dear boy, I fancy you,' she whispered in my ear as she grabbed my bum and pulled me towards her. 'It is the champagne which always has this effect on me.'

'Gosh, Lizzie,' I stammered as her finger stole round to rub against my swelling penis. 'Does this mean you want, to, um, I mean, would you like to, er — '

'Oh very well, you persuasive young man,' she laughed. 'You've talked me into letting you fuck me.'

With those words she stuck her tongue in my mouth and, showing commendable dexterity, unbuttoned my fly to release my erect prick which was straining against the confines of my trousers. She pulled me down upon the bed and took as much of my cock in her mouth as she could, stroking my staff with one hand and teasing my testicles with the other. Somehow we managed to strip off all our clothes and we rolled over as she spread her creamy thighs. I buried my lips in her buttery bush and as I licked her, I ran my thumb into her cunney and this drove her absolutely wild. She grabbed my hair and pushed my head back into her curly motte. 'Eat me!' she commanded and a few moments later her cunney was grinding down on me as her juices soaked my face.

By now my balls were aching and I needed to spend. Lizzie anointed my thick young flagpole with her wonderfully wet tongue and then climbed aboard for a ride. Guiding my cock into her cunt, she leaned over so that her big, stalky red nipples brushed my chest. I have a mirror on the wall opposite my bed and it was unbelievably erotic watching us fuck. All too quickly I spurted a huge flood of spunk inside her as she bucked to and fro on my sturdy pole, reaching, as the first jets of spunk hit her cunney walls, a truly shattering orgasm.

My cock was still hard so Lizzie took hold of my wiggling prick which was sticking high in the air and rubbed my knob in the vale between her large titties with their deep red nipples. Then, kneeling before me, she slung my legs over her shoulders and taking my stalk in her hands, began to tongue my hairy ballsack. Then she moved up to embrace my knob with her lips. She opened her mouth and sucked in my shaft until it touched her throat. Oh, how I loved being sucked off! Up and down, up and down bobbed her head, until, with a low growl, she changed the steady movements into an erotic circling pattern until I could stand it no longer. I bent forward until I was almost doubled-up and shouted: 'I'm going to shoot, Lizzie! Do you want it in your mouth or in your cunt?'

She pushed me back and before I could spend, she sprung back and laid herself on the bed, encouraging me to throw myself upon her in the most ardent terms. She threw her legs over my back and we commenced a short sharp bout of the most enjoyable fucking. The muscles of her cunney tightened gloriously around my shaft as, with a gigantic whoosh, the white froth burst out from me, hot and seething, into her eager nook. Gush after gush spurted uncontrollably deep inside her as Lizzie happily screamed out that her own climax was upon her and our cum juices mingled as we came together in a glorious mutual spend.

We could both have wished to continue but, alas, Lizzie had promised to rejoin her friends on the charabanc back to their hall of learning. But we have arranged to see each other again during the summer. She lives eighty or so miles from my home but it is a journey I would happily make by foot if necessary for another hour with Lizzie, an honours graduate in *l'arte de faire l'amour.*

I have the honour to be, Sir,
Your Humble Servant,

Clive Kiniston-Jones
Belsize House
The Grove
Norwich
June, 1890

The Editor replies: You do not say whether the young lady has completed her studies. If she has not and requires employment during the long summer vacation, do not hesitate to pass my address to her.

THE REMARKABLE ADVENTURES OF PORLOCK HOLMES

'Unless I am very much mistaken,' said the great detective, 'we are about to have a visitor. A woman of some standing in society who has just enjoyed a prolonged and vigorous bout of sexual congress.'

'How on earth do you know that?' I asked, amazed at his powers of prediction.

He beckoned me over to the drawing room window. 'Note the carriage standing at the kerb outside the house,' he said. 'It drew up some three quarters of an hour ago. Since then, no one has emerged. You will observe also that it is a private equipage, well maintained and with a discreet monogram on the door. The blinds are down and it has been swaying rhythmically on its springs ever since it first arrived. In my experience that is a sure sign that the occupants are engrossed in the noble sport of fucking.

'Had they been involved in a fight, the movements would not have been nearly so regular and had the parties not been mutually eager for their encounter the duration of their activities would have been considerably shorter. Only a willing couple could have kept up the engagement for such a period of time.'

'Good God, Holmes,' I said. 'You continue to surprise me.'

'Simple observation,' he said. 'You are not, I take it, of a musical disposition? The tempo of their movements, as far as I could judge by the bouncing of the carriage, moved from *lento* to *andante*, modulated to *allegro* and then built up inexorably to a thrilling *furioso*, before subsiding once again by stages to *lento*.' He fingered the strings of his violin as he spoke and gazed down into the street.

'Notice also the horse,' he said. 'It became somewhat

'Notice also the horse,' he said. 'It became somewhat agitated while the bout was at its most animated. The coachman had to hold its head as it attempted to back between the shafts. Even now its nostrils are flared and it is tossing its mane.

'Animals frequently respond with great excitement in the presence of human intercourse.'

I suppose that I had never properly considered this point before, but now I came to think on it, I recalled at least two occasions when the household cat had leaped upon the bed with a great purring and head-butting while I was in the process of grappling with one or other of Mrs P – 's daughters. Indeed I remembered Hannah, or was it Becky, bursting out in a fit of giggles as she attempted to push the persistent animal away as it tried to squeeze itself between our bodies.

'Come,' said Holmes, dragging my attention back to the present, 'We must prepare for our guest. Whatever her purpose in calling on us, she will be in sore need of something comfortable on which to recline. The sofa, I think. Help me spread this rug and pile up some cushions for her.'

Moments later the front door bell sounded and I heard the housekeeper shuffle down the hallway. Footsteps ascended the stairs and there came a quiet knock at the drawing room door.

'A lady to see you, Sir,' said Mrs Sayers, a gaunt woman who seldom if ever smiled but was fierce in her devotion to her employer. 'She prefers not to give her name but insists that you will be pleased to receive her.'

'Show her in, Mrs Sayers,' said Holmes.

As he said this, the door was pushed fully open and there entered an extremely handsome woman dressed in the height of fashion. Her bosom, a delightfully full bosom I could not fail to observe, rose and fell as though she was considerably out of breath. Her veil was flung back to reveal a pair of sparkling eyes with a faraway, dreamy look in them. Her lips were parted and her skin deliciously flushed.

As the door closed behind her, our visitor looked round in some state of agitation, then her glance fell on me and she started, backing away as though to leave the room.

'I had thought that you were alone,' she said to Holmes.

'My dear Lady M –,' he began.

'How . . . did you know my name?' she gasped.

'Suffice it to say that a trained eye and a trained memory are among the basic skills needed in my profession, while your face is not unknown in Society.'

Still exhibiting every sign of alarm, she looked questioningly in my direction.

'My assistant, Mr Andrew Scott,' said Holmes. 'I can assure you of his complete discretion. Everything you say will be in absolute confidence.'

As I rose to be introduced, I felt a familiar stirring as Mr Pego rose also, eager for his part for his own introduction to this enticing creature. I noticed that the all-seeing Holmes had spotted the tell-tale bulge in my trousers. One eyebrow was raised quizzically but he spared my embarrassment by keeping a straight face.

'Mr Holmes,' said our visitor, 'forgive me for my presumption in bursting in on you unannounced but the matter is urgent. I am being blackmailed.'

'By your husband, I suspect, Ma'am,' said the detective.

'How – how on earth did you deduce that?' she said with a little gasp of surprise.

'Elementary, my dear Lady M – ' he replied. 'You arrived in your own carriage. I have it on good authority that your husband is away on an official but secret mission to the Hapsburg Court concerning the recent unrest in the Balkans. Hence your dalliance at my doorstep has been with a man other than your spouse. I would add that your husband is well known for his enthusiasm for the science of photography.' He walked over to the bureau and produced a flat package from a pigeon hole. 'Indeed these are examples of his recent endeavours.'

Our visitor let out a little cry of distress and subsided in tears upon the sofa. 'Where . . . where did you get them?' she asked between sobs.

'My dear, you must pull yourself together,' said Holmes. 'Scott, there is brandy in that cabinet, and glasses. Lady M – is in need of a restorative. Help yourself as well.'

'And a glass for you?' I asked.

'My pipe will suffice,' he answered, reaching for the lady's laced boot on the mantel in which I had learned he kept the unusual smoking mixture he preferred and which was provided for him by a villainous-looking Lascar seaman who called clandestinely at regular intervals.

He tamped the mixture down in his pipe, struck a lucifer and inhaled deeply. 'Aaah, the Orient brings us many pleasures,' he murmured. 'But now, to the business in hand.'

Our visitor dabbed delicately at her eyes with a flimsy handkerchief, swallowed her brandy and mutely held out her glass for replenishment. As I bent to pour another libation, I caught the tantalising scent of a woman who, whatever her present distress, had but recently been wholeheartedly engaged in the pleasures of the flesh. Mr Pego gave another twitch. At once a warm, ungloved hand reached out and settled on the protruding source of my passions. She gave an unthinking little squeeze before realising what she was doing.

'I'm sorry,' she said pulling back from my aroused member. 'I hardly know what I am about. But thank you for your attentions.'

'Lady M — ' said Holmes, drawing on his pipe, 'We have here a most unusual coincidence. These photographs were handed to me in the strictest confidence by your husband. He asked me to discover the identity of the parties involved. With your permission, I would like to show them to my assistant. He is not inexperienced in such matters. You have my word, and his, that this matter will be handled in utter secrecy.'

'Indeed, yes,' I said, although truth to tell, I had not the slightest idea of what was depicted in this substantial portfolio of likenesses. 'I shall be the soul of discretion.'

'I can see that I will have to trust you both,' said Lady M — as a deep blush spread over her face. 'But I hope that you will not think too badly of me.'

'If I may speak frankly,' said Holmes, 'I have little other than contempt for many of the public conventions of the age. Providing only that such activities are not carried out in the street where they may frighten the horses, they are largely to be encouraged. I am talking,' he said, turning to me, 'of fucking.'

Somewhat bemused by the turn of events, I could but stammer out my agreement. His opinions after all differed not one iota from those of my old headmaster, Dr White.

'But blackmail,' he continued, 'is the most loathsome of crimes. You are, Lady M– , a woman of considerable independent fortune, are you not? A fortune rather greater than that of your husband, particularly since he has lately been speculating rather unwisely in companies trading with the Baltic States and St Petersburg.'

'Indeed, yes,' she answered. 'His finances are now precarious in the extreme and he has become increasingly pressing in his suggestions that I should make over a substantial part of my capital to him so that he can avoid ruin.'

'But you have been thus far adamant in your refusal,' said Holmes.

'I have been for some years supporting a Home for Fallen Women as well as a retreat for disgraced and unfrocked clergymen, while much of the estate is entailed.

'My attorney tells me that legally I am bound to surrender all that I have to my husband if he so demands,' she continued. 'But this I will not do unless he forces the issue through the courts.'

'You do not like your husband, I take it?' said Holmes.

'Ours has not been a happy marriage,' she said. 'He is cold and domineering, obsessed with his position in Society and often unfeeling in his demands on me. For several years I have had to seek affection beyond the bonds of marriage.'

'And this search for affection has now led you to the point where he or some other who wishes you ill, has evidence that can destroy you in the eyes of the public,' said Holmes.

'Worse. He has already stated that he could have me put away in an asylum for the insane. Yet mine are surely the most natural of appetites.'

Again, an anxious hand reached out for me and clutched at my out-thrust manhood so convulsively that I flinched, fearing some damage to that most sensitive part of my anatomy.

'Ow!' I said.

'Oh, I am sorry,' she said. 'I have inadvertently hurt you. Here, let me kiss it better.'

My heart seemed to swell with pity and affection for this poor creature in distress. I vowed that I would do whatever was in my power to soothe her urgent needs. As I drew myself up to my full height and prepared a gallant speech to that effect, she unbuttoned me and my prick fairly leapt out into plain view. At once she lowered her head and gently enclosed its straining head with her lips. She licked eagerly at its tip before releasing me for a moment. 'You have a most understanding assistant, Mr Holmes,' she said.

'There are in fact considerable limits to his powers of understanding,' said Holmes, rather unfairly I thought, 'but his heart, and indeed his other organs, seem to be in the right place.'

She bent her head once more and without more ado took my whole swollen length into her mouth, sucking and nibbling with such expert concentration that I rapidly forgot the knotty problem that she had presented us with. I decided that I would leave the more cerebral aspects of the case to Holmes. He was already poring over the photographs, tapping the mouthpiece of his pipe against his teeth, his brow wrinkled with concentration.

'There are several members represented here,' he said. 'One I believe I can put a name to. Two, I believe may come from North of the Border. Another should be easily discovered since he has only one testicle, and this one,' he gestured towards it with his pipe, 'has a curious tattoo of a Masonic nature on the foreskin.' He scrutinised the print. 'I shall need my magnifying glass. I believe you may be sitting on it, Ma'am.'

'Wfffllll, oooffl, gluppp,' she said, unable to speak with her mouth full.

Holmes looked at our visitor with a slight gesture of impatience.

'If I might prevail upon you to disengage yourself from my assistant, Ma'am, I must ask you some questions.'

With a guilty start, our delightful visitor withdrew her lips that had been so energetically sucking and teasing at the by now greatly swollen head and shaft of my member. I must have made some involuntary gesture of disappointment for I had been but moments away from discharging the full contents of my throbbing testicles down the length of my cock and into that warm, receptive mouth. Realising my distress, she took hold of Mr Pego in her hand and slipped one of her gloves on to him.

'I am sorry,' she said, 'but we have to attend to the subject of my visit. This will at least keep him warm until I am able to resume my ministrations. I know that it is unfair in the extreme to leave a man in such a state of expectation.'

How thoughtful she was, I thought to myself, although her kind action had left me in a rather delicate social dilemma. It would be ungallant to remove a lady's glove when it had been so understandingly pressed upon me, yet I could not easily thrust prick and glove together back inside my trousers. I realised that I should have to leave my unusually ornamented member protruding *en plein air* while I played my part in the consultation that was about to begin.

'Let us first consider whether the blackmailer is in fact your husband and not some other scoundrel who has gained access to the evidence of your extra-marital adventures,' said Holmes. 'May I ask you, Ma'am, to describe in detail the circumstances of the delivery of the threat.'

'Some three weeks ago,' said Lady M — , 'a large envelope was presented at the front door by a street urchin. He announced to my maid that he had been handed the package by a man he had never seen before, along with tuppence, and told to ensure that it was delivered to me personally, and that it contained documents of a strictly private nature and was to be opened by no-one but myself.'

'An impertinent demand,' said Holmes. 'But do you recall anything distinctive about your visitor?'

'He was an urchin like any other,' Lady M — replied. 'Badly dressed in hand-me-downs and clearly a stranger to soap and water.'

'And did you not ask about the stranger who had entrusted him with the errand?'

'Why, no,' she said hesitantly. 'You will understand that I am not unaccustomed to the clandestine delivery of *billets doux* and letters of assignation.'

'Of course,' said Holmes. 'Given the nature and, may I say, the complexity of your extra-domestic arrangements, such anonymous missives must arrive with some regularity.'

'That is so,' she said with a quick smile as she dropped her eyes in modesty. Unfortunately this caused her gaze to fasten upon my gloved member and she gave a little giggle. A consolatory hand reached out and, like a devout Catholic playing unconsciously with her rosary beads, she began to fiddle with me. Some instinct, most probably of neatness, led her to smooth the glove along my ramrod so that the head was forced into the opening of the middle finger of the glove. Such an entry was of course impossible and as the thin fabric stretched in its unachievable task of containment, I realised that if she continued with this course of action, however pleasant, some damage to the seams of the thin silk of her glove would inevitably be done.

I closed my hand over hers in warning. She ceased her stroking and pulling but continued to hold on to the tip between her thumb and first finger. Absent-mindedly she continued to toy with it, as though seeking some assurance.

At this juncture, Holmes smacked the dottle out of his pipe against the fender and held it out in my direction. 'A two pipe problem,' he said. 'If you would be so good as to replenish it. A generous filling, and packed well down.'

As I prised my prick somewhat reluctantly from the hands of Lady M — and her gentle kneadings, I took the proffered pipe and began to stuff it with the sweet-smelling oriental mixture.

'Now,' said Holmes, 'the note. Do you still have it?'

'I have brought it with me,' said Lady M — , 'together with the enclosures.'

'Enclosures?' said Holmes.

'A set of pictures that would appear to be duplicates of those that you have received. Although I have of course had but the briefest glimpse of your set.'

'May I inspect the note first of all,' said Holmes.

She reached into her reticule and drew out a well-folded piece of paper.

'An obviously disguised hand,' said Holmes, 'but clearly that of a man of some education, correct in the spelling and grammatical construction. We are not dealing with some working class fellow from the criminal classes.'

'A man?' I asked. 'How can you tell?'

'You will find in the library a monograph on the science of handwriting,' he said a little impatiently. 'Written by myself, it was, in all modesty, well received by the Society of Calligraphers when I presented it at their annual conference. The fruits of a lifetime's study. I have conclusively demonstrated that the gender, class and much of the character of any individual can be deduced from a careful examination of even the smallest sample of a script.

'I have attempted long and fruitlessly, I am sorry to say, to engage the interest of those clodhopping asses at Scotland Yard in my researches. It could in many cases be a valuable aid to detection. You may recall the Case of the One-Armed Plenipotentiary where I was able to render some small service to the forces of law and order. The Home Secretary of the time was rightfully very grateful and a discreet Honour was subsequently bestowed on me at a private investiture by Her Majesty. Not that I set any store by such baubles. The successful application of the Intellect in the solution of any problem is satisfaction enough, I find.'

I could not but notice that a note close to self-satisfaction had crept into his voice. Lady M — was also growing a little restless as he reminisced. She caught my eye, smiled, and fingered the top buttons of her dress in a most provocative fashion. As she drew a deep breath, her enticing bosom rose so that the shadowed valley between her creamy, plump titties was exposed. Mr Pego, who had been showing some signs of relaxing, re-erected in an instant.

Meanwhile Holmes took a deep suck at his pipe, drawing the smoke down into his lungs and holding it there. His eyes closed as though in a trance. 'Aaarrrgh,' he murmured as he exhaled. 'I feel my mental processes at work.'

Lady M — reached out and took my hand in hers. She

raised it to her lips and moistened a fingertip before inserting it deep down the front of her barely buttoned bodice and placing it on the unseen nipple that rose unhesitatingly to my touch. Gently I rubbed it and felt it hard and fat against my skin. She leaned forward so that her breast nestled in my cupped hand. I squeezed it carefully, trying not to disturb Holmes' cerebral concentration.

Holmes began to read, at first to himself but then out loud.

"'If you wish to retain your place in polite society, you will recognise, dear Lady M —, that it would be greatly to your advantage to obtain possession, not only of these prints but of the original photographic plates. These can be delivered to you with complete discretion at any time that you may choose. We both understand that the greatest care must be taken to ensure that they do not fall into the hands of any third party, in particular the editor of one of the public prints, nor, it goes without saying, of your husband.

"'There will of course be certain unavoidable expenses in order to assure both safe delivery of the originals and to ensure my continued silence in the matter.'"

Holmes read on silently. Lady M — had frozen at his words, my hand still clamped firmly on her breast. I essayed a tentative squeeze to show my sympathy with her plight but she did not react. Mr Pego, sensitive as ever to the nuances of the situation, lowered his head. Holmes read on, once more out loud.

'The transfer of a very substantial amount of money will be necessary.'

Lady M — bowed her head and a tear trickled down her cheek. I pulled her glove off my prick and handed it to her so that she could mop her eyes. She sniffed.

'Thank you Mr — ?' she said.

'Scott,' I said. 'Andrew Scott.'

'Thank you, Andrew,' she said. 'You are most sympathetic.' She turned to Holmes. 'The sum demanded,' she said, 'will come close to beggaring me.'

She stood up suddenly and began to pace the room, unconscious that her splendid bosom was spilling out of her dress. So abrupt had been her movement that I fell forward on my knees, Mr Pego flopping on to the carpet as a milky bead of cum hung suspended from his tip. Holmes noticed.

'The rug is Turkish,' he said. 'From a village close to the Persian border. The same area from which I obtain my smoking mixture. I would be grateful if you can avoid staining it. It is very precious. The only other is in the Victoria and Albert Museum.'

I scooped my member up and wiped it with Lady M – 's discarded glove. 'My apologies,' I said, but Holmes' attention was once more directed to the matter of the blackmailing letter.

'But the money can be raised?' he went on.

'Just,' she said.

'Which suggests either that this is an improbable coincidence or that the demand comes from someone with an intimate knowledge of your financial affairs. We are dealing with a well-informed scoundrel. I notice however that there is no mention of the means by which these funds are to be transferred.'

'If you read on,' said Lady M –, 'you will see that he promises a further communication. All I am asked to do at this juncture is to assent in principle to his demands. A messenger is to call for my reply at some time in the next week.'

'Then we must be present also,' said Holmes.

'But he enjoins the strictest confidence,' she said.

'Never fear,' said Holmes, 'we shall be nearby but unnoticed when the agent of this diabolical plot arrives.'

'How will you ensure that?' she asked. 'The time is not stated. You might, I suppose, be lodged in my household.'

'That, alas, would be most unwise,' said Holmes. 'The arrival of two male guests while your husband is absent abroad would certainly be noticed in the neighbourhood. All my experience confirms that servants are inveterate gossips. Very little escapes their eyes and everything that is noticed becomes the subject of tittle-tattle amongst all their fellows in the vicinity. That is why I make the point of keeping the smallest establishment possible. Mrs Sayers is the soul of discretion while Mr Scott here will already have noticed that the boy and the maids speak only Portuguese: a language not generally understood in this country. I interviewed them all personally whilst in Oporto two years ago, where I was solving the Case of the Adulterated Wine.'

As with Colonel Moore (*see Oyster 2, 3,* and *4*), I realised that I was in the habit of falling in with men prone to digression.

'So what will we do?' I asked, dragging him back from triumphs past to problems present.

'That we will discuss later,' he said. 'But a scheme is forming in my mind. Rest assured, Lady M — that when the messenger returns, we will be present and observing all that transpires, although I suspect that you will not be aware of us.'

'So you are convinced that this vile plot is definitely all the work of my husband?' said Lady M — .

'In all probability,' said Holmes, 'although we must not discount the possibility that two separate attempts are being made to divest you of your fortune.'

'How horrible,' she said. 'I am ever too trusting of human nature.'

'And also somewhat careless with your affairs, Ma'am,' said Holmes. 'I would in future counsel some care in the bestowal of your favours.'

'I will try,' said our visitor, 'but you must understand that I am not one of your blue-stockinged, intellectual modern women. To put it bluntly, I have needs that have to be satisfied.'

'You like fucking,' said Holmes, bluntly.

'It is I suppose my chief enjoyment in life,' she said, drawing herself up to her full height and looking him straight in the eye.

'But until this frightful business is cleared up, I do most strongly suggest that you are, if not wholly continent, at least careful. Take for instance the gentleman who is waiting for you outside in your carriage.'

'An old friend,' she said. 'One who I can trust.'

'Will he not be becoming bored with the wait?' I asked.

'I suspect not,' Lady M — said with a roguish grin. 'He was

well drained from his exertions when I left him. He deserves some rest. But how did you know of his presence?'

'You were observed,' said Holmes. 'Or rather the vigorous motion of your carriage was observed.'

Lady M— blushed. 'I was so nervous concerning my visit to you that Matthew decided that I needed to have my mind taken off my plight for a few minutes.'

'Three quarters of an hour,' said Holmes.

'Good Gracious! Was it that long? How time does fly when one is fucking. Anyway, I did feel much better afterwards. But now I am beginning to feel rather tense.' Again she involuntarily reached out and clutched my member. I winced.

'Oh, sorry!' she said. 'I've squeezed you too hard.'

'Not at all,' I said, blinking a little as tears sprang to my eyes. She relaxed her grip and began to caress my prick with regular but gentle strokes. All the pain was quickly soothed away and it thrust boldly out once more.

'If you feel the need of some further relaxing exercise,' said Holmes, 'pray do not hesitate. I am certain that Scott will help you and I need to ponder some more on what is to be done.'

'That is very understanding of you,' she said. 'If Andrew is prepared to help a lady in distress — '

'By all means,' I answered, delighted at the realisation that I could actually help Holmes in his professional endeavours while at the same time assisting this poor suffering creature to gain some semblance of relief. 'Anything I can do to ease your anguish,' I said.

'I suggest that you ease your prick into my pussey,' she said with that commendable directness of expression that so often marks the upper *echelons* of our society. 'Now, off with your trousers!'

I did as I was told. She fairly threw herself backward upon the cushions, pulled up her dress and raised her knees. Without more ado, I lowered myself on to her.

Lady M— was clearly thoroughly experienced in such matters. There was none of that clumsy bumping and boring that so often attends the fumbling embraces of the novice. Mr Pego immediately slipped through the already damp thickets of her pussey hair and found the moist entrance to her cave of delights. At his touch, she wriggled her bum into a more comfortable position and opened up before me. Almost without effort, the entire length of my prick sank into her up to the hilt. I paused as she tightened her grip on me and a smile of pure pleasure lit up her face.

'That is just what I need,' she said, holding me for a moment or two.

Slowly I began to slide easily up and down her warmly clinging cunney. She in turn began to rise to meet my thrusting. Like any gentleman, I endeavoured to keep my weight on my elbows and, intent though I was on my delightful task, I could not help but notice that Holmes, not one whit put out by the scene that was being enacted in front of him, was scrutinising the photographic prints he held out before him. At one point he peered intently at some detail on a print using a magnifying glass. Then he screwed a monocle into place, raised his head and stared at Lady M – 's private parts now fully revealed as her dress rode up over her stomach with its deep-set navel.

'A memorable bush,' he murmured to himself. 'And a certain identification.'

Meanwhile the pace of our efforts had been increasing. It was as though we had fucked many times before. Our breathing was in unison, deeper now as a slight sheen of sweat oiled our bodies. My prick tingled with the firm pressure of her inner walls. We fitted together as though a benign Providence had designed each for the other.

Now she lifted up her legs still further and crossed them behind my waist, pressing me down into her, yet she did not grasp me so tightly as to inhibit my rhythm. We speeded up and then with a natural control, relaxed our efforts a little. Again our efforts increased and again slowed down. She had a wonderful sense of timing, understanding as though by instinct when to lower the tension so that our pleasure might be prolonged.

Holmes meanwhile had taken a pair of callipers from a desk drawer and was taking careful measurements from the photographs, noting down the results in a small book. His brow was a little furrowed as he concentrated on his task but there was a slight smile of satisfaction on his lips. Then he looked around him.

'Scott, could you — ' he began and then pulled himself together, realising that I was far too buried in my own work to assist him. 'I am sorry,' he said, 'Do carry on.'

We did indeed carry on. Lady M — had in any case clearly not heard his half-swallowed remarks. She was absolutely absorbed in our joint venture. Throughout our whole fuck she concentrated entirely on her pleasure and mine. Without any sense of artifice or unnatural effort, she both responded to my needs and attended to her own. She was of that admirable school of thought that holds that fucking is an activity for two. There was no mindless surrender to her own desires at the expense of my own. Nor was there any watchful deference to my will or possible demands such as is found in some of the more professional ladies that I have encountered.

So we fucked for a considerable time, locked together as one. Yet gradually the intensity of our activities increased. Each renewed level in tempo took us one step towards the final climax. From an easy canter, the pace was raised to a full yet sustainable gallop. I wondered at my own stamina. I was dimly aware that outside dusk must be falling as Holmes, with the thoughtful man's true patience, continued with his own intellectual efforts but allowed Mrs Sayers into the room to move softly about, lighting the gas and attending to the fire.

Then the rate of our striking increased still further as I drove in and out of my ever-responsive companion. Somewhere in the hallway I was aware of a clock chiming. At that moment I felt the first pulsation as my balls began to release what was to prove a veritable tidal wave of cum. As it began to flood unstoppably down my cock, I sensed that she also had reached that same point of abandonment to our bodily demands. It was as though she widened, opening out to receive my libations as they jetted time and time again into her. She did not cry out but moaned softly, then suddenly caught her breath. She matched my every surge as though she also was discharging her cum into me. But still there was no

109

sense of desperation but rather a feeling of inevitability as tide met tide and mingled in one rush and whirlpool of coming. So completely taken up was I by our climax that I swear the house could have burnt down without my noticing. Each jet felt now as though it must surely be the last, yet time and time again I felt one further eruption churning inside me. I was panting and shuddering as though I was emptying my entire being into her.

Then, imperceptibly, the pace began to slacken. Amazingly, we did not stop. There was no final exhausted thrust. No sudden collapse. Smoothly but inevitably we slowed, both breathing deeply, relaxing gently, still responding each to the other. Both of us began to be more aware of our surroundings. She turned her head to one side, a look of complete satisfaction and fulfilment spreading over her face.

'Stay inside me,' she said quietly. 'I can still feel you.' Then she hugged me to her, tucking her head into my shoulder. A last quiver of mixed emotion and cum flowed from me and we held each other silently.

'Forty-seven minutes,' said Holmes, fishing out a half hunter from his waistcoat pocket. 'A remarkable performance. I suggest a brandy, when you have disentangled yourselves.'

'I did not realise that we were being timed,' I said, a little put out by his attentions.

'Purely in the interests of Science,' said Holmes. 'The scientific measurement of all manifestations of human activity is one of my particular areas of intellectual endeavour. Alas, there has been as yet little published statistical evidence of the duration range of human sexual congress. A lack that I hope to remedy in a paper that I am preparing for private circulation within the next eighteen months. The evidence that I have collected so far is most interesting. One minute is the shortest time I have recorded. Yours was one of the more prolonged encounters I have been able to witness. However explorers in the East claim that four hours or more of *coitus uninterruptus* is regularly achieved among the adepts of some of the mystic sects of Tibet.'

'An indoor record, I imagine,' I said.

'A record but not necessarily indoors,' he replied. 'Well over two hours in a snow drift in the foothills of the Himalayas has been observed.'

'Both parties being well wrapped up?' said Lady M — , beginning to take an interest in the conversation.

'Stark naked, in fact,' said Holmes. 'Both of them.'

'Who was on top?' asked Lady M — .

'They changed positions several times,' said Holmes. 'The most fascinating fact is that none of the snow melted. It seems that through long training, they were able to retain all their body heat and concentrate exclusively on their exertions.'

'Amazing!' I said.

'On the contrary,' said Holmes. 'Through life-long spiritual immersion in the arts of Yoga, the *swamis*, as they are called, can attain complete control of all their bodily functions.'

'Like those pictures of old men with long beards, sitting on beds of nails and feeling no pain,' I said.

'But do they ever fuck on beds of nails?' asked Lady M — .

'Only the most advanced initiates,' said Holmes. 'There are dangers of course.'

'I shall stick to beds and sofas and carpets,' said Lady M — .

'And carriages,' I added, remembering the long session that Holmes at least had viewed from the window.

'I have tried it on a croquet lawn,' she went on. 'But we bent two of the hoops in our efforts.'

'But the hoops at croquet are set some considerable distance apart,' said Holmes thoughtfully. 'I must consult the rules for the correct spacing.'

'It was a rolling fuck,' said Lady M — . 'We did do some damage to the turf as I recall.'

'There was not a game actually in progress at the time, I assume?' I said.

'At the beginning,' said Lady M — . 'I have a distinct recollection of being struck by a croquet ball quite early on in our encounter, but then the other parties fell to fucking as well. Except for the bishop.'

'A bishop!' I exclaimed.

'I remember looking up and seeing a pair of clerical gaiters at my head, and above them a large pectoral cross dangling over a purple-clad paunch.'

'And was nothing said?' I asked.

'Nothing at the time,' she said. 'Although I recall afterwards that there was something of an atmosphere over tea. Meaningful looks exchanged over the scones. That sort of thing. Of course the silly man should have joined in instead of trying to play on and ending up losing his balls in the shrubbery.'

'What!' I said.

'Well, nearly,' said Lady M — . 'He became entangled in a snare that had been set by one of the keepers.'

'Shooting and sex,' said Holmes. 'The preoccupations of the Landed Gentry through the ages. However, we must return to the subject of your visit, Lady M — . A plan is beginning to form in my mind.'

I should at this point explain the rather unusual circumstances that had led to my acting as the temporary assistant to Mr Porlock Holmes who readers will recognise as being the greatest amateur detective of our age.

Mrs P — , the widow in whose house I lodged in Bayswater, had as I have previously mentioned in my memoirs (*see Oyster 2*), a considerable interest in certain aspects of the Classical and Oriental Arts. She was, for instance, one of a small group of *cognoscenti* who had long been urging Mr Richard Burton, the noted explorer, to translate into English such eastern texts as the *Perfumed Garden* and the *Karma Sutra*. She engaged in frequent and detailed correspondence with a learned circle of scholars of the erotic. In addition one of her daughters, Hannah, was an artist and potter of growing repute as well as being, along with her sister, a frequent partner of mine in the amatory arts. She was particularly interested in recreating the styles and techniques of some of the more unrestrained early Greek ceramic artists.

It happened one evening, just as I was looking forward to one of our regular postprandial entertainments of a sexual nature, involving Hannah, her sister Becky and in all probability several of their friends, that Mrs P — announced towards the end of dinner that her friend Mr Porlock Holmes was interested in commissioning from Hannah a substantial vase, to be decorated with some scene from Greek mythology.

'What subject does he have in mind?' asked Hannah.

'He is as yet undecided,' her mother answered. 'Indeed he is prepared to be guided by you in the matter. He did though mention various subjects including Europa and the Bull and Prometheus Condemned to Eternal Punishment.'

'What about Leda and the Swan?' suggested Hannah.

'My grounding in the Greek myths is, I regret, uncertain,' I said.

'A constant theme,' said Mrs P —, 'is that of one of the Gods, in most cases Zeus, descending in various guises and surprising some hapless nymph or sprite and then leaping on her with great gusto. The unfortunate Leda was one such unwilling object of his attentions.'

'For the occasion, he took the form of a large swan,' said Hannah.

'What was the outcome?' I asked.

'An egg, or eggs,' said her mother. 'One hatched into the twins Castor and Pollux.'

'And according to some authorities of Antiquity, the fair Helen was also the fruit of their union,' Hannah added.

'That would seem a thoroughly suitable subject,' said Becky. 'I would be more than happy to pose as Leda. I see myself down on all fours, possibly looking at my reflection in the water and wearing something diaphanous in white.'

As I pictured the scene I began to see a part for myself.

'I would be more than happy to surprise you in such a position,' I offered.

'I don't doubt it,' said Becky. 'But you would have to be covered with feathers.'

'With his arms outstretched like wings,' said Hannah, clearly visualising the scene.'

'And a beak,' said Becky with a teasing smile.

'And webbed feet,' added her sister. I sensed a note of ridicule creeping into the conversation.

113

'Let us ring for cook,' said Becky. 'I know that she is intending to serve up a goose for tomorrow's dinner. I saw the poulterer delivering a large, well-feathered bird earlier today.'

By now I was beginning to have second thoughts about the whole endeavour but before I could protest, cook was summoned to confirm her plans. Moments later I found myself down in the kitchen, face to face with a substantial dead specimen of *Anser Domesticus*.

'Just the thing,' said Hannah, seized with enthusiasm. 'We shall pluck it immediately.'

'I, in the meantime, will go and pick out some suitable drapery,' said Becky.

'Give cook a hand,' said Hannah to me.

'Plucking is not one of my skills,' I said hastily.

'Then you must learn,' said Hannah firmly. 'First the plucking and then the fucking. You cannot take part in one without the other.'

'Don't worry, Mr Andrew,' said cook. 'Just watch what I do and follow me.'

Thus it was that some ten minutes later I found myself holding a stripped and naked bird while a stripped and naked Becky crouched invitingly in front of me.

'Are you certain that you will be able to perform to the satisfaction both of my sister and myself?'

'I have never failed yet,' I answered, my pride somewhat hurt.

'That is true,' said Becky. 'But in this case you will have to exercise a considerable degree of self-control. Several sessions will be necessary, so that my sister can sketch the tableau to her satisfaction. Are you sure that you will be able to hold your position without moving. Here!'

In an instant I had been forced down onto one knee while my arms were stretched out like wings. Becky and Hannah, quite ignoring my protestations, pushed and pulled me this way and that, standing back at intervals to scrutinise the effect.

'Right hand down a bit,' said Hannah. 'Can you get him to bend forward a little more.'

'Let's try him standing up and bending forward,' said Becky, dragging me to my feet.

'Legs a little apart,' said her sister. 'He's a bit stiff.'

'He frequently is,' said Becky with a grin. 'But not all over.'

The fact of the matter was that I was being so manipulated and shoved around that Mr Pego was at his most shrivelled and limp. This to my chagrin was revealed when both sisters began to divest me of all my clothing. Both looked sorrowfully at my state.

'Upstairs,' said Becky. 'At least it will be warmer, and I would prefer carpet rather than stone flags under me.'

Clutching a bowl of feathers, I was urged up the stairs. Once in the drawing room before a blazing fire, I felt more at ease. Hannah went off to bring her crayons and sketch pad, while Becky began to try various nymph-like positions in front of me. As she raised up her delicious bum, Mr Pego awoke from his slumber and jutted out in front of me. Unable to resist what was spread out before me, I dropped to a kneeling position behind her and with my hands on her hips, drew her to me. The tip of my prick slid easily between her thighs and began to probe at the entry to her lovely cunney.

'Can you keep it just like that,' said Hannah as she suddenly came into the room. I groaned with frustration and moved forward another inch or so.

'Don't let him in, Hannah,' said Becky. 'In this instance Nature must wait upon Art.'

'*I* seem to be suffering for *your* Art,' I said, a little bitterly, but, I thought, rather cleverly.

'Come out of my sister at once,' said Hannah, failing completely to respond to my witticism.

Becky it was who took pity on me. 'Later, Andrew,' she said, 'I can promise you an absolutely splendid fuck. And no doubt my sister can be prevailed upon to join in our activities. See, already I am quite damp with anticipation of what is to come. But now you must be greased and feathered. Arms out.'

Accepting my fate, I stood up. I was liberally smeared with what seemed to be lard, and first the down and then a selection of large wing feathers was pressed on to me. At this point both Becky and Hannah burst out laughing.

'Not at all like a Greek God,' said one.

'More like a scarecrow,' said the other.

At this point I became quite angry. 'You are making fun of me,' I said, making as though to leave the room.

'Come back at once,' said Hannah. 'Don't be so stuffy. See, we can all join in.' With that she slapped a pat of lard or butter on her sister's bared bottom and threw the rest of the feathers at her so that they stuck to her all over. Becky gave a squeal of protest and pulled at her sister's dress. In a trice they were wrestling over and over on the rug in a great confusion of discarded clothing and sticky feathers.

'Mr Porlock Holmes,' announced Emily the maid, suddenly appearing at the door. 'Shall I show him in?'

'The Library,' said Becky, choking with laughter and a mouthful of fluff. 'Mother will entertain him, at least until we are more presentable.'

So it was that a few minutes later I made my first acquaintance with the world's greatest detective. He was sitting at a desk in the library, smoking the oddly smelling pipe that I was later to come to know so well. Mrs P — was beside him and together they were poring over a large volume of what I later discovered to be Etruscan drawings.

'Mr. Scott,' said Mrs P — as he looked up. 'He is presently staying with us. He is aware of the commission that you have in mind and has kindly offered to help in any way he can.'

'He is to be our Swan,' said Hannah. 'Although up to now he had not numbered bird impressions among his repertoire.'

'*Cygnus olor*, *gibbus* or *mansuetus*, the Mute Swan,' said our learned guest. 'A graceful creature, if one of uncertain temper. You are familiar with the genus *Cygnus* of the family *Anatidae*?'

'I have seen them swimming about,' I said. 'But must admit that I have not studied their habits in depth.'

'I am certain that the Misses P — will complete your education. As an artist, Hannah is well trained in observation while Becky has a nurse's interest in anatomy,' he said. 'I look forward to seeing the first sketches in due course but will not intrude on your work. I have, in any case, a small problem on which Mrs P — can in all probability give me the benefit of her considerable learning. The case I talk of,' he said, turning to his hostess, 'is that of the Incontinent Cabinet Minister. A matter of great delicacy for I fear that the Irish Question has raised its ever-importunate head. I sense a Fenian plot.'

'How much I regret the failure of Mr Gladstone's Home Rule Bill,' I said, determined to demonstrate to the great man that I had a sound grasp of the political issues of our time.

'He once accosted me in the street,' said Becky. 'I believe that he mistook me for one of his Fallen Women.'

'It is important for a man to have some interest in his life other than his work,' said Holmes. 'Even a Prime Minister. I myself, apart from my musical endeavours, am particularly interested in the problems posed by the employment of barmaids in many of our public houses. On the one hand it is argued that they are in a position of obvious moral danger, working as they do in close proximity to both men and strong liquors. On the other, the barmaid is in a situation, unusual particularly among working class women, of being able to dictate the behaviour of men. She can, for instance, refuse to serve any fellow who is being rowdy or objectionable. She can even order him out of the premises. So the question is raised as to whether the opportunities outweigh the dangers.

'Of course, in the interests of the Science of Detection, I have from time to time to enter, usually in disguise, many of the vilest drinking dens in the poorest parts of our city. It was on one such visit that I first became interested in the problem. I was, if I recall aright, at that time engaged on the Case of the Jaundiced Debutante, at the instigation of her mother, the Marchioness of Bolsover. But I am becoming indiscreet.'

He turned to Mrs P — . 'Have you a large-scale map of the County of Sligo in Ireland?' he asked. 'I must return to my intellectual labours and you to your artistic endeavours.'

Becky, Hannah and myself, thus dismissed, returned to the drawing room where Becky and I at once removed our clothing and I was greased and feathered before being pushed and patted into position, hovering, more like a vulture than a swan, as Hannah said, over Becky's invitingly bared bottom.

Hannah sketched industriously away. I was driven to shut my eyes in order to resist the temptation that stared me in the face. Crouching as I was with arms outstretched, down on one knee and with my eyes tight shut, I found it extraordinarily difficult to keep my balance. My plight was not helped when Becky could not resist the temptation to inch backwards so that I could feel the cleft of her buttocks pressing lightly against the tip of my engorged prick.

Hannah did not help matters. 'A little further forward,' she said. 'Can you open yourself up a bit, Becky.'

The strain was too much for me. Carefully I half opened one eye. Becky had reached back and with both hands had pulled her cheeks apart. Her tight little arsehole was flaunted, scarcely half an inch from my cock.

'He's peeking!' said Hannah to her sister. 'Supposing he was to enter just a little way into you. You could hold him fast in position and he could keep his balance. Don't drop your arms,' she said to me sharply. 'I'll arrange things.' She moved over to me and took my prick firmly in her hand.

'I've got it lined up,' she said to her sister. 'Just ease your way backwards on to him.'

Becky shuffled backwards and I inched my way into her.

'That's enough,' said Hannah. 'Now, hang on tight.'

'He's a bit big,' said Becky.

'Goose grease,' said Hannah. 'That will do the trick.' Carefully she smeared some of the by now warm fat on my cock. 'Try again,' she said.

This time I slid smoothly into her. Becky released her grip on her bum cheeks and as they closed about me, I was held fast.

'Just like that,' said Hannah. 'That's just about right. Andrew, you're sagging!' I must have looked surprised for seldom if ever had Mr Pego been more proudly erect.

'Your arms,' said Hannah, recognising my confusion. 'It's your arms. They're drooping.' She pulled both arms upwards so that I looked more like some great bird of prey swooping down on its victim. She stood back and scrutinised the scene that she had arranged.

'That will have to do,' she said and retreated to her sketch pad.

'I'm tired,' I said, for the strain on my shoulders was beginning to tell.

'We could prop him up,' said Hannah. 'I'll get one of the maids to bring up a couple of pieces of wood.'

'Like splints,' said Becky. 'We have been taught how to do that in the hospital. Andrew, you can relax for a minute or two until we get this fixed up.' With a sigh of relief I let my aching arms drop and at the same time surreptitiously pushed forward. Becky wriggled her bum and all of a sudden I had measured my full length into her. She let out a little yelp of pleasure and settled herself once more, gripping me round the base of my swollen member. I gritted my teeth and tried to keep control of myself.

It was in this position that Emily the maid found us when she answered the bell.

'This is Art,' said Hannah firmly to her. Instructions were issued to the startled servant. Two broomsticks were procured and bound firmly to my arms. The ends were jammed rather uncomfortably into my armpits while the heads, a mop in one case and a stiff yard broom in the other, projected out beyond my fingers' ends. Two chairs were propped under my splinted arms. Becky remained in position, clasping me warmly in her bum. I had seldom if ever felt so foolish. The situation was not improved when Emily stepped back from her handiwork and burst out laughing. At once she was all confusion and embarrassment.

'I'm sorry, Miss Hannah,' she said. 'But he does look so funny.'

Hannah joined in the laughter, clutching at Emily as they both gave way to complete hysterics. Becky also began to choke with uncontrollable giggles and the vibrations so teased my prick that I found myself being squeezed and teased to a point where I could no longer control myself. I began to thrust backwards and forwards into her. Becky, her head cradled in her arms, began to react as her desire for a good bum fucking fought with her determination to help her sister in her classical efforts.

119

With my arms still pinioned and propped, I was now driving energetically into Becky's eagerly responding bum. Suddenly one chair overbalanced and I half fell over sideways in a clatter of furniture. Becky reared up and I collapsed on to her, one wing sticking up in the air and the other trailing on the ground like a hen partridge feigning injury. So slippery were Becky and I with the now melting grease that only her tightly clamped sphincter prevented my complete downfall.

'How Athenian,' said a male voice. Unnoticed, Porlock Holmes had entered the room.

'A most interesting situation,' he said. Stepping forward, he set the overturned chair upright once more and set me on an even keel with each arm once more supported. Becky's succulent titties were still heaving and trembling with her half-stifled laughter. Fastidiously, he wiped the grease from his hands on the crumpled piece of drapery that had long since fallen off Becky's naked body. With his head set on one side he eyed his handiwork before arranging the thin material over her body. Seemingly satisfied, he seated himself at the table and took out his pipe.

'Mr Scott,' he said, 'I have a proposition for you. My assistant Dr Motson has had to leave the country for a few weeks. Some fuss with the governing body of the Royal College of Physicians. I regret that he has made enemies among the senior members of his Profession. Some trumped up charge involving medical ethics following his invaluable assistance to me in the Case of the Pregnant Mother Superior. It will all doubtless blow over as these things do, but meanwhile, I am without his help. I mentioned my problem to the good Lady of the House and she suggested that you might be interested in taking over Dr Motson's duties for a short while. She assures me that you have handled at least one delicate errand for her, concerning, I believe, Rosie, the Errant Schoolgirl and she further describes you as adaptable and resourceful.'

'He has indeed proved himself able and willing to rise to the occasion whatever has taken place in our house,' volunteered Hannah, rather nicely I thought.

'If a little clumsily,' added Becky, *sotto voce* from her

position on the carpet. She pushed backwards over-vigorously and I fell off my perch once more. She remained impaled on me and as I tried to scramble back into my classical pose, pushed again so that I fell over backwards, she sitting on my upthrust manhood. Holmes appeared to take no notice of the flailing and tumbling that was going on under his eyes. Swatting a couple of floating feathers away from his face, he sucked on his pipe and I smelt the exotic fumes with which I was later to grow so familiar.

It was in these unusual circumstances that I became the temporary assistant to the Greatest Detective of our Age. I had never before been offered employment while lying flat on my back with a naked woman speared on my prick, but my old headmaster had long since impressed on his pupils that opportunities must be seized with both hands, even if, as in this case, both hands were strapped to broomsticks. I assented to his interesting offer and arrangements were made for my new employment.

'I look forward to seeing the outcome of your artistic imagination,' Holmes said to Hannah courteously. Emily fetched his cape and rather odd hat and he made his Goodbyes. Prometheus was Unbound and we fucked merrily on the carpet, Hannah putting away her drawing materials and joining in, although not before she and Emily had thoroughly sponged down both her sister and I.

Two days later I was delivered, bag and baggage, to Porlock Holmes' rooms in a house close to the Metropolitan Railway Company's station on the Marylebone Road.

A further week and my involvement in the Case of the Blackmailed Wife was underway. I was impersonating a crossing sweeper and keeping watch on all who called at a house in Belgrave Square.

'What happened to the usual crossing sweeper?' asked the fellow in livery.

For a moment I was minded to tell him sharply that it was none of his business, but then remembered that I must behave according to my subservient situation. Holmes had taken up his duties early that morning and had instructed me firmly that I was to take over from him at midday.

'Every visitor to Lady M—'s Belgrave Square establishment is to be noted,' he had said. 'In particular any errand boy and member of the servant class must be regarded with suspicion. All we know is that a message is to be delivered from the blackmailer during the course of this week.'

Becky and Hannah, who had been made partially privy to my task, had fitted me out in an ill-fitting, shabby set of clothes, enlisting the services of Mary the maid.

Holmes, for his part, had been so thoroughly disguised that I had completely failed to recognise him when I presented myself at the street corner at the ordained time.

'Pssst!' A chesty but tremulous voice had whispered as I cast about me. He had entered thoroughly into the spirit of the adventure. Instead of the upright, elegant figure that I had come to know, a crabbed, bent creature approached me. Using all his theatrical skills, he had contrived a hare lip and the mottled complexion of one who spends too much of his time and money in sordid drinking dens.

I caught a pungent whiff of sweat and horse manure as he murmured his instructions in my ear. I recoiled as though by instinct from this stained, consumptively coughing figure.

'Scott!' he said urgently. 'It is I! Take this broom. I have to return to my rooms. I shall return later in the afternoon, around half past four. I have here a list of the regular callers, together with details of their appearance. If Lady M— has the opportunity to alert you, her lady's maid will appear at the window at the left hand side of the first floor. If you see her signal, you are to follow anyone not of the household who leaves.'

'Supposing he does not set off on foot?' I asked.

'There is a cab waiting round the corner. The driver is a reliable man whom I have used on many such occasions. He will do exactly as you say,' said Holmes. 'On no account are you to lose our quarry. If you are not present when I return, I shall assume that you are in hot pursuit. When you have some news, you are to return at once to my rooms, no matter what the hour.'

I had been engaged in my simulated employment for about an hour when this inquisitive servant accosted me.

'Old George is not well,' I said, remembering my script. 'His leg is troubling him more than usual. My uncle and I are taking it in turns to carry out his functions until he is recovered.'

'That would be the decrepid creature whom I saw this morning,' said the fellow. 'Don't go away. My mistress may have an errand for you.' With that, he turned on his heel and disappeared down the steps of one of the houses adjoining Lady M – 's.

This left me in something of a quandary since I could not desert my post without incurring the wrath of Holmes. However, I could hardly protest without my interlocutor becoming suspicious. I could but hope that his mistress would not have need of my services.

My hopes were to be dashed. Scarcely ten minutes had gone by when he returned.

'You are to come with me,' he said. 'My mistress needs your services.' He strode off haughtily without giving me the opportunity to demur. Reluctantly I tailed behind him. We went in through the servants' entrance and I was taken into a hallway and then upstairs, through a baize-covered door into the family's part of the house.

'In here!' he ordered brusquely, 'And wait. You will be given your instructions shortly. Nothing is to be made dirty.' Here he wrinkled his nose with disgust. 'Remain standing. The silver is all counted.'

I half opened my mouth in order to damn him for his impertinence when I recalled that I must, at all costs, remain in my character as a member of the lowest orders. I tugged at my forelock with a dirt-stained hand and cringed.

'Of course, Sir,' I said. 'I hope I know my place.'

He eyed me disdainfully, turned and left the room. I stood there, inwardly cursing my luck that had taken me from my observation station. As I stood at the window, the door opened and what was clearly the lady of the house swept in. She halted and ran an imperious eye over me.

'You're a thoroughly dirty fellow,' she said. 'And rather younger than the old man who performed this morning's duties.'

Obviously Holmes had also been dragged in from the street, although he had said nothing of this when I took over from him.

'My uncle, Ma'am,' I said.

'I hope you prove to be somewhat more vigorous in the discharge of your duties. He wheezed most horribly and indeed had to be revived by cook with a bowl of soup.'

Well-preserved would be the phrase that best described her. She was of middling age and height and full-bodied, tending a little to the stout.

'Now,' she said brusquely, 'I want you to enter me from behind!'

To my amazement she lifted her dress and leaned over an occasional table. A well-fleshed pair of buttocks was presented to my astonished gaze. Beneath the cleft I could see a dense, dark bush. She opened her legs a little and pulled apart her splendid cheeks.

'Come along,' she said. 'In there!'

I paused, still reluctant to obey her command.

'What are you waiting for,' she said.

Gingerly, I approached her, very aware of my grubby condition.

'It don't matter about the dirt,' she said. 'I want your hand on me and your cock in me. Get it out at once!'

Bemused, I did as I was told. Mr Pego hesitantly revealed himself. She looked at it.

'That won't do,' she said. 'Stick it between my legs. I see that I shall have to bring you to life.'

Cautiously I introduced my member to the indicated position. At once her thighs closed and she began to rub and coax it with a considerable degree of expertise. At her warm, skilled touch, my cock swelled and rose.

'That's better,' she said. She reached round behind her to grasp him in her hand.

'Much better,' she said. 'Big and hard, that's how I like it. Now, embrace me.'

'Beg Pardon, Ma'am,' I said. 'But I'm not very clean.'

'That's why I sent for you,' she said. 'I want to feel your hands on me.'

I grasped her tentatively, my hands on her hips.

'The waist, and then further up,' she ordered.

I did as I was told. Mr Pego at least declared his interest in these goings-on. Still with a degree of caution, I seized hold of her clearly voluptuous breasts, squeezing them and pressing them through her dress.

'Better,' she said. 'You're learning fast.' She began to breathe heavily and her own hands crushed mine against her. Her bared buttocks began to thrust and move against me. Mr Pego was by now rampant and I began to slip backwards and forwards between her firmly fleshed thighs. She began to twist this way and that.

'Push my clothes up,' she ordered, releasing her grip on my hands.

By now I was beginning to be quite carried away with my efforts. Sliding my hands up her thighs, I raised her dress well above her hips. My hands moved higher and encountered the large breasts which were quite unencumbered with any underthings. Again she gasped and then fairly threw herself forwards across the table so that her bum stuck proudly up in the air.

'Now!' she said and my engorged prick slipped directly into the opening of her cunney. She backed and forced herself along the full extent of my shaft. At once we fell to a completely abandoned bout of fucking. As I forced my way time and again into her, a little trickle of sweat made its way down her back and into the cleft. I rubbed my face eagerly in it. As she felt the stubble of my unshaven chin scratch her naked flesh she began to give out low groans of pleasure. By now the immaculate state of her clothing was becoming not just creased but torn. My begrimed fingers had left distinct prints on her damp-sheened body. Her hair was in a state of wild disorder. For my part I had been able to step neatly out of my trousers as they threatened to tangle round my ankles.

'More! More!' she cried out.

Ceaselessly I banged in and out of her now wide and wet cunt. My balls felt full to bursting but I attempted to control the eruption that was building to its climax. Drawing on all my experience, I first slowed down and then increased my pace. All of a sudden I felt the first unstoppable wave of my cum beginning to force its way down my prick. Before I had time to do anything, she had noticed what was about to happen.

'You're coming,' she said. 'Not inside me!' She bundled up the hem of her dress and used it like a handkerchief, wrapping it round the head of my prick just as the first milky spurt shot out. With one hand reaching down between her legs, she held me tightly as jet after jet was emptied into this hastily devised rag receptacle. I had been full to overflowing and soon my cum was smeared over her hand and seeping down her thighs. With an experienced hand she ran her fingers along my prick, urging every last drop of my spending out of me.

'Well done,' she said, as my discharge dwindled to nothing. Letting go of me, she twisted round and lowered her head to my still out-thrust member. With one mighty suck she emptied the last few drops and then, as my prick began to relax, she took it into her mouth in its entirety so that it lay along her tongue. She let it rest there, holding me firmly at the hips. Then, as Mr Pego shrank back to a more manageable state and size, she let me go.

'But I have not yet come,' she said. 'You must complete the job with your tongue.' She lay down on the carpet, quite oblivious to the mess that we were making, parted her legs once more and revealed the full splendour of her bush to me.

I kneeled before her and she reached out and pulled my head between her knees. Needing no further instruction, I at once began to feel my way with my mouth through the luxuriant undergrowth that hid her cave of delights. Already gaping and wet, her cunney lips welcomed me in. My tongue at once encountered the fullness of her clit which moments before I had been teasing into vigorous life with the thrusting of my prick. I began to lick it with quick, darting strokes. She rolled her hips, widening herself out under my attentions. The warmth of her pussey hair filled my nostrils and I breathed in the scent of her own coming.

By now she was crying out loud in a quite uncontrollable manner. A first shudder and then a second announced that she was reaching the final point of her ecstasy. Her bosom bounced up and down as she bucked and heaved like some thoroughbred trying to dismount its rider. I held on to her manfully however, my tongue clinging to her clit like a barebacked rider. Gasp after gasp forced its way from her and I was quite enveloped in the tides of her coming.

Soon her volcanic movements began to subside but not before I swear I felt the floorboards move and groan beneath us. Still panting with her exertions, she ceased all movement for a moment or two. Then she pushed my head away and drew her legs up with surprising flexibility for one of her age and build. With her own hands clamped firmly against her pubic parts, she rocked back and forth, a great smile of satisfaction spreading over her face.

'Very good,' she said. 'Very good indeed. Much better than your uncle.' So at least I had surpassed Holmes in one thing, I thought with satisfaction. I should call this the Case of the Satisfied Pussey. One that I had brought to a triumphant conclusion without any help from my mentor. Then I remembered that I had failed in my duties as observer at Lady M — 's. What would Holmes say? At once, I decided that since he had said nothing to me about the services he had been called on to render during his spell on watch, I was under no obligation to volunteer any description of the similarly unexpected summons that had drawn me away from my street-sweeping duties.

'Ring for the maid,' Her Ladyship ordered in her customary imperious tone.

'But . . . but . . . ' I stammered. 'Don't you need to, er . . . ?'

'Get on with it, young man,' she said. 'Abigail has been with me for years.'

I did as I was ordered. No doubt, I thought to myself, the maid must be used to such scenes, extraordinary though they might seem to most people. And indeed the maid Abigail, when she answered, behaved as though it were the most natural thing in the world to find her mistress, half-naked, dampened and considerably dirtied, stretched out full length on the carpet while a ragged but untrousered member of the lower orders stood by the bell.

'If you would like to gather your things together,' she said to me. I collected myself up, adjusted my dress and followed her out of the room. Her Ladyship barely looked up.

'Take him out by the kitchen entrance,' she said. 'But he may have a wash first at the sink if he wants.'

Once outside, the maid said 'Her Ladyship would like you to take this as a reward for your efforts.'

With that, she slipped a half-sovereign into my hand. This was the first time that I had ever been offered money for satisfying a lady and for a moment I resisted. But then I remembered my assumed status and accepted my payment. 'The Labourer is Worthy of His Hire' was a proverb I recalled from my school scripture lessons.

'Her Ladyship is well satisfied,' said Abigail as I completed a perfunctory wash. 'She will in all probability send for you again. In addition, while there can be no question of a written reference, there is every likelihood that she will recommend you to Mrs Lucas across the street. She also has need of occasional assistance in these matters, seeing as how her husband is so often away on business.'

'I had no idea that this sort of thing went on,' I said.

'It's not for the likes of us to concern ourselves with the habits of the gentry,' said Abigail rather sniffily. 'Though I must say that I prefer my gentlemen callers to be clean at least.'

Thus dismissed, I returned to my duties at the street corner, hoping that there had been no need for my other clandestine services while I had been away. Cautiously, I looked across to Lady M — 's. All appeared to be as it had been. I fingered the half-sovereign in my pocket, hoping that there would be no further demands upon my time and energies.

About an hour later, Holmes returned.

'I take it that nothing of note has transpired,' he said.

'Er, no,' I said, a little worried that he might have returned while I had been called away and was testing my veracity.

'A completely uneventful spell?' he asked. Was it just my guilty conscience or did he suspect something.

'No unexpected callers at Lady M — 's,' I said, aware that I was being evasive. I spotted a raised eyebrow.

'I, er — ' Then I pulled myself together, remembering that he also had been plucked from his observation station to render the self-same service as myself. 'Honesty is surprisingly often the best policy,' had been one of the maxims most favoured by Dr White at Nottsgrove.

'I had to leave my post for a short while in order to answer a call of nature,' I said, edging towards a full confession.

'Your nature or another's?' asked Holmes with a thin smile. He had guessed. With a sense of relief, I admitted to my adventure. He listened.

'It's a damn nuisance,' he said when I had finished. 'I sometimes forget the demands of the flesh. I also received a similar call earlier.'

'You don't think that the woman is in league with our blackmailer and that it was done deliberately to draw us away from our vigil?' I suggested.

He pondered the point. 'Possible but not probable,' he said. 'Although of course, a neighbour would have every opportunity to observe the comings and goings at Lady M — 's. Discretion is clearly not among her more marked qualities. There is nothing for it. Tomorrow we will both have to be on duty at the same time, in case further calls are made upon your services.'

'Or indeed, yours,' I said.

'I suspect that I shall be spared the wretched woman's demands. I had the foresight to simulate considerable incompetence.'

For a moment I entertained the unworthy thought that his incompetence had not been deliberate but then remembered that he was an adept in the more demanding Oriental arts.

'At least I shall remain in a position to carry out our watching brief,' he went on.

'Two crossing sweepers?' I said. 'Will that not look a little odd.'

'You shall be the sweeper,' he said. 'I shall remain completely hidden.'

'How?' I asked.

'I am an expert in these matters,' he said. 'Never fear. I will be invisible but present.'

'In the meantime,' I said, 'how long are we to remain here?'

'All night, if needs be,' Holmes said. 'The criminal classes have a natural affinity with the hours of darkness.'

I began to have some doubts about the pleasures of the detective's life. Dusk was falling. A cold wind was beginning to blow and my ragged clothing was likely to prove quite inadequate in keeping out the nocturnal chill. I was also becoming extremely hungry.

'I wonder — ' I began.

'Ssssh,' Holmes said, holding up a warning finger.

'What?' I said.

'That tapping noise,' said Holmes.

I strained my ears. Sure enough, from some distance but nearing rapidly there came a sound of shuffling footsteps accompanied by a strange, insistent rapping.

'A blind man,' I said as I discerned a figure approaching in the gloom.

'Making surprisingly swift progress for one with his affliction,' said Holmes. 'Something's afoot.' Suddenly he turned in the other direction.

'A second blind man,' he said. 'An odd coincidence.'

We ducked down some area steps as he motioned me to silence. The two figures converged, each feeling along the kerbstone with his cane. Closer and closer they came. With a bump and a mutual cry of surprise, they collided. Each stood still as though waiting for the other to step out of the way. Then each began to mutter angrily as they measured up to each other. One waved his cane and made contact with the other.

'This is awful,' I whispered. Each obviously assumed that the other could see and expected him to stand aside. In a trice they were swearing and flailing at each other. I stepped forward.

Holmes pulled me back. 'Don't,' he hissed, 'I scent a diversionary tactic.' By now a grotesque fight had broken out. A carriage pulled up and the driver leaped down to pull the two apart. A passer-by joined in.

'There!' said Holmes.

'What?' I said.

'There! Getting out of the far side of the carriage.' Sure enough a shadowy figure had slipped out and quickly vanished towards the servants entrance to Lady M—'s establishment. 'That's our man,' said Holmes. 'Keep down!'

'How can you tell?' I asked.

'A well-dressed man in a top hat and with a silver-topped cane, descending to the *servants* entrance,' said Holmes. 'Even the most superior servant would not be so dressed. Note also the military bearing.'

There came the softest of raps at the door. At once it opened and our quarry was let in.

'Someone was waiting for him,' said Holmes. 'There is an accomplice inside the household.'

'What do we do?' I asked.

'We wait,' said Holmes.

We waited. The fighting blind men allowed themselves to be parted. They calmed down and tapped on down the road. The coach driver remounted, clicked his tongue at the horse and proceeded on his way, turning the corner and passing out of our sight. The passer-by, who had been the accidental recipient of a couple of stinging blows, patted himself down, wiped his face and walked on, limping a little. Silence fell. Holmes began to creep up the steps. Then as I followed, he crouched down, and I felt a pull at my elbow from behind. I turned, startled.

'Tuppence for a fuck,' said a small voice. 'Or thruppence for the both of you.' Angrily I pulled away.

'Not now!' I exclaimed, trying to keep my voice down.

'Tuppence for a very good fuck,' she insisted, and two thin but strong arms were flung round me. 'First of the evening,' she importuned. 'A good clean fuck.'

131

As I tried to wrestle her from me, my foot slipped and I fell down the steps and landed in a heap at the bottom, all entangled with her. As her body was squashed under mine, she wriggled and hung on to me.

At this point Mr Pego betrayed me and rose to attention. She felt my mutinous member pressing against her and quickly dropped her hands down, seizing hold of him through the unfortunately threadbare cloth of my disguise.

'My, he's a big, strong fellow,' she said. 'Surely you wouldn't deny a girl a chance of feeling that inside her.'

Despairingly I looked up but Holmes had vanished, leaving me to grapple with my seductress.

'Never mind about the other gentleman,' she said. 'You can catch him up in a minute or two.'

'He's not a gentleman,' I hissed. 'We're just a couple of poor crossing sweepers. You've made a mistake.'

'Crossing sweepers don't talk like that,' she said. 'You're gentry, no matter how you're dressed. On your way to a fancy dress ball, are you?'

'We're keeping watch — ' I started, nearly revealing all in my confusion.

'Never mind what you're doing,' she said. 'None of my business. In here!' She pushed open a door and dragged me into complete darkness. Something gave way under my feet and I fell over once more. There was a rumbling noise and what felt like a cascade of stones fell on me.

'We're in a coal hole!' I cried out, trying to regain my balance but falling over again as the mound of coal shifted under me. 'This is ridiculous!'

'Never mind,' she said, quite invisible in the Stygian blackness but still keeping firm hold of my prick. 'The dirt'll just add to your disguise. Now keep still while I get my gloves off. Don't want to get your prick all gritty. I'll have him out in an instant.'

Strong little hands unbuttoned me. As my eyes began to get used to the darkness, I could just about see my prick, ghostly white where the light from the half-closed door caught it.

'There,' she whispered. 'I'll guide you.'

All at once I felt the warmth of her bush rubbing against the tip of my already straining member. I stopped struggling. What else could I do? The quicker we got this over, the quicker I could get out and follow Holmes.

Now she was straddling me as I lay back. Expertly she lowered herself on to my prick, burying it entirely in her already wet cunney. Cautiously she began to ride up and down on me. I responded and felt the coal shift beneath me.

'Careful,' she said. 'We don't want to start an avalanche.'

I lay still once more. The idea of being buried alive while fucking did not appeal. She did not make any abrupt movements but just used her inside muscles, clenching and unclenching herself about my swollen cock. 'Cleopatra's grip,' I recalled Becky calling it. One of those feminine skills handed down from Antiquity in a centuries-old tradition. Never was it more needed now. One over-abrupt movement and catastrophe threatened.

Perilous though our situation was, I realised that I was beginning to thoroughly enjoy it. I was in the hands, or rather the cunney, of an expert.

As I surrendered to professional care, I forgot everything except the delicious rhythmic squeezing that was rapidly driving me towards my coming. I felt the first stirring as my jism began to churn inside my swollen balls. I must have made some slight sound.

'That's it,' she said, 'let it come. Everything you've got. Right into me.' I did as I was bid. Steadying myself on the ever-shifting coal slope with my outstretched arms, I began to pump spurt after spurt of my cum up and into her. After the events of the afternoon, I was surprised at how much I could summon up. Rising and falling a little now on me, she milked me as our juices were spread over my prick and began to trickle down into my hair.

'I call it my Wishing Well,' she said softly in my ear. 'When the last drop comes out, you must close your eyes and think of what you would most like to happen to you. I can see the whites of your eyes,' she went on. 'You're supposed to close 'em when you wish.'

I did as she commanded. All I could wish was that I could

get out of there as soon as possible and follow Holmes. My first Case and already I had a sense of failure.

'All done then?' she said.

I nodded and then coughed as some coal dust tickled my throat.

'Up we come then,' she said, carefully lifting herself off my discharged but still erect firing piece. 'A good two penn'orth, wasn't it?'

I nodded again, feeling in my pocket for some coins. As I began to lever myself up, I slipped.

'Blast this coal!' I said.

'Anthracite,' she said.

'What?' I said, still struggling to pick myself up.

'Good Welsh anthracite,' she said. 'Best there is for burning. Born and brought up in the Valleys, I was. Learned my trade at the pit head.'

'Young woman, this is not the time or place to discuss the merits of different types of coal,' I said, looking up at her. 'Help me up!'

She reached down, seized hold of my hands and pulled me to my feet.

'I must find my friend,' I said.

'I'll come with you,' she said. 'Maybe he'll want a quick fuck as well.'

'I think you'll find that he has other things on his mind,' I said, rummaging round in my pocket for the money to pay her off. My fingers closed round something. 'Here, take this!'

As she took the only coin I could find in my hurry, I realised from the milled edge that it was in fact the half-sovereign with which I had earlier been paid off after my own afternoon endeavours. However it was too late to take it back. Already she had hidden it about her person. For a moment I considered asking for my change but realised that as a Tuppenny Upright, she was hardly likely to have enough cash on her to be able to comply with such a request. I made a mental resolve to be more careful with money in the future.

'Now we must set out after your friend,' she said, yanking me out into the evening gloom. I saw a small smile flit across her face as she realised the extent of her luck and my mistake.

At least, I consoled myself, it would appear that I had a higher market value.

My immediate problem was to track Holmes down. Carefully I climbed up the area steps, my Welsh Undresser, as I had Christened her in my mind, rather wittily I considered, followed close behind. The road above was empty. I started across.

All at once there came a terrible moaning noise. 'My God!' I muttered out loud. 'Holmes!' He must have been attacked by the well-dressed fellow we had seen admitted to the servants entrance. I began to run towards the sound.

The door was still ajar and speedily but quietly I slipped inside, knowing not what scene of outrage I might find. The room was empty but through an open door and from down the passage, the unearthly moaning recommenced. I looked around wildly. Obviously Holmes must be in terrible trouble. If I was to be of any use to him, a weapon was needed. My eye lit upon a large rolling pin and I picked it up, feeling its reassuring weight in my hands.

'I don't think that will be needed, dearie,' said a small Welsh voice. I looked round. My Tuppenny Upright had followed me in.

'I must save my friend,' I said, rather impressed by my own heroism. 'Stay out of the way. This is man's work.'

'Woman's,' she said, contradicting me.

'What?' I said.

'It's all right,' she said. 'I know that sound — '

'Shhh!' I said, pulling away from her as she tugged at my sleeve.

'But — ' she said, refusing to let go so that I found myself dragging her in my wake as I raised the rolling pin and began to creep towards the bloodcurdling sound. I finally just about managed to shake her off but she insisted on following me, ignore her though I might.

The first two rooms we came to both had partly opened doors. There was no lighting but I realised that one was a larder and the other a store of some kind. The moaning sound came from ahead. I pressed cautiously on. All of a sudden my foot caught what appeared in the half-light to be a

135

scrubbing brush. It skated across the stone flags and clanged against a bucket. As the sound echoed down the passage, the moaning came to an abrupt end. An ominous silence fell and then there came the patter of hasty footsteps. Casting caution to the winds, I rushed on. We came to a right-angled turn. I paused and edged forward. Another room opened off the corridor. Flattening myself against the wall, I inched my way onwards, trying to keep myself concealed until I could get a clear view through the doorway. From behind came a stifled, choking sound. I spun on my heel. My companion had her hand to her mouth.

'Shhh!' I said again. Again I paused, gathered up my reserves of courage and then fairly leaped in, ready to do battle.

'About time, too,' came a quiet voice.

'Holmes!' I cried out.

Holmes it was. He was standing by a small window, upright and wound about with what seemed to be a large sheet, his arms bound to his sides like an Egyptian mummy. He was pulling rather crossly at the ends of his imprisoning bandage which had been fed between the rollers of a large mangle.

'What — ' I exclaimed.

'The handle,' he said.

I strode across the room, seized the handle and quickly gave it a couple of brisk turns.

'The other way!' my employer cried out in a strangled voice. 'You're pulling me through the wringer!'

'Here, let me!' said my partner from the coal hole. 'I can see you've never been in service.'

She took the handle from me, reversed my efforts and began to release the Great Detective from his bondage.

'Now,' she said, as the ends were freed. 'You take one end and I'll take the other.' She laughed. 'Like a maypole. We've got to unwind him. Go round that way.' Obeying her, I set off clockwise. Ducking under my arms, she circled round in the opposite direction. Holmes, trying to help us, began to swivel round.

136

'It would be quicker, Sir,' she said, 'If you stayed still. We'll have you out of that in a trice.'

He did as he was told and with a few quick turns we had him disentangled. He stood there, swaying slightly on his feet.

'He's a bit dizzy,' she said. 'We'll turn him round the other way. That way he'll get his balance back.'

'You realise, of course, that these childish games are in fact connected with ancient fertility rites,' said Holmes, ever the teacher.

'Just what my old headmaster used to point out to us,' I responded, pleased to be able to demonstrate my knowledge of such things. 'I had not realised, Sir, that you had a particular interest in folklore.'

'A longtime but minor interest,' he said. 'Though one that has been useful to me before now in my detective work.'

I remembered the moaning and the sounds of hasty departure that had preceded our entrance, although all was now quiet.

'What happened?' I asked.

'As you should be able to deduce,' said Holmes, 'I have been assaulted in a most disgraceful fashion. They went that way,' he continued, pointing down the passage that stretched further ahead.

'How many were there?' I asked.

'Three,' he replied. 'One was the fellow we had been following. Or rather, *I* followed. You seem to have been somewhat delayed on the way. I notice also,' he said, 'that you appear also to have acquired a companion.'

'Er, this is er — ' realising as I began my introduction that of course I had no idea whatsoever of the name of my Welsh Encounter.

'Megan, Sir,' she said. 'Do you want a fuck? Only fourpence.'

'My dear young lady,' said Holmes, 'Grateful though I am for your assistance in releasing me, you must realise that this is neither the time nor the place for such a transaction. Evil is afoot and we must be in hot pursuit.'

'Did you get a good look at the other two?' I asked, somewhat concerned at the prospect of a hand-to-hand

137

engagement with no less than three opponents. For a moment Holmes appeared embarrassed.

'They were women.' Uncharacteristically he hesitated. 'Both substantially built and both, er, both stark naked.'

'Good God!' I exclaimed.

'Two large naked women. Probably of the servant class, judging by their coarse hands and coarse language.'

'What were they doing?' I asked.

'Behaving in a manner not dissimilar to that suggested by your friend here,' he said. 'They were accompanied in their activities by the well-dressed stranger.'

'Why did they tie you up?' asked Megan. Once more Holmes looked crestfallen.

'I had managed to approach the door, which was then half-closed, unnoticed,' he said. 'Believing from the noise that some foul crime was being perpetrated, I bent to observe what was going on through the crack between door and frame. Unfortunately, at that very moment, one of them looked up from their revels on the floor — '

'So *that* was the noise,' I said, enlightenment dawning.'

'If I might make so bold,' said Megan, 'that's what we in the trade call a screaming fuck.'

Holmes looked startled but I remembered the tremendous racket that had been set up by Mary the Maid at Mrs P — 's at the hands, or rather instrument, of Tom the Tool (*see Oyster 2*).

'I should have recognised it,' I said ruefully.

' — they looked up,' said Holmes, pressing on testily, 'and let out a great cry of "Peeping Tom!" Before I could either escape or explain myself, I had been roughly laid hold of, bound up in two large damp sheets and fed into the mangle.'

'How terrible!' I said.

All at once there came a spluttering sound. We both turned to see Megan bent over with laughter and pointing to the linen. As a consequence of our assignation in the coal cellar, there were now dozens of large black handprints all over the twisted remains of the sheets.

'They denounced me, using the foulest possible expletives,'

Holmes continued, clearly unamused by the turn of events. 'And then fled.'

'We must catch them,' I said.

'Why?' asked Megan.

'Because they have criminally attacked Mr Holmes,' I said. 'And the full rigour of the law must be visited upon them.'

'I concur with your sense of outrage,' said Holmes, 'But I have reservations as to your suggested course of action. Not only would they have some semblance of a defence in court but I should have to explain why I had been apparently spying on their perfectly legal sport. Such publicity would not help me in my endeavours to apprehend the blackmailing swine who is the cause of so much distress to Lady M.'

I could see the logic of his argument. 'But what then do we do?' I asked.

'May I remind you, Scott, that we are actually in the basement of Lady M – 's house. I suggest that we seek her out and find out if there have been any further developments in the affair while I have been unavoidably detained down here.'

'But what if we inadvertently happen upon your assailants?' I asked.

'I do not think we have to fear any further attack,' he said. 'Not only are we now their equal in numbers, but I strongly suspect that the two women will be chiefly concerned to reclaim their clothes and resume their domestic duties. As for the fellow, I would imagine that he has been either hidden away or pushed out into the street again.'

'Unless they hope to complete their fucking,' said Megan.

'That is a rather remote possibility,' said Holmes. 'We do not I think need unduly to concern ourselves with them any longer.'

'So we'd better go and look for Lady M – without further ado,' I said.

'May I remind you that we are both dressed as crossing sweepers,' said Holmes. 'I suggest that if we suddenly appeared before her looking like this, she might well become considerably upset. Also your friend here is not suitably dressed for a lady's drawing room.'

'I knew you wasn't a real crossing sweeper,' said Megan. 'A fancy dress ball is what I suggested if you recall.'

'Very observant of you, my dear,' said Holmes. 'You have the makings of a detective. It may be that I shall enlist your services. I would of course make it worth your while.' He fished out a small purse. 'Sixpence would seem an adequate sum for your services.'

'Make it ninepence and I will throw in a free fuck,' said Megan.

'That won't be necessary,' said Holmes. 'Although Mr Scott here might well be interested in your offer at some time later on.'

'He's already had his fuck,' she said.

'Which doubtless accounts for the delay in his arrival.' He turned to me. 'Scott, I am not unappreciative of your efforts to stand in for Dr Motson, but you might be more useful to me if you could remember to use your head rather than your balls from time to time.'

'Bit of a prick on wheels, is he?' said Megan brightly.

'Ah, yes, an army expression, is it not,' said Holmes. 'You have experience of the military?'

'The Barrackroom Bint of Blaenau Festiniog, I was known as at home,' she said. 'And then I served the Navy at Portsmouth before coming to London.'

'So you have considerable experience of the foibles and predelictions of humanity,' said Holmes. 'A veritable student of society.'

'I can tell the difference between a gentleman and a crossing sweeper,' she said quickly, 'However he may be turned out.'

'We must have a long talk together at some time in the future,' said Holmes. 'There are questions that I should like to put to you. Knowledge,' he said to me, 'must be sought in all quarters, even the most unlikely. But in the meantime, there is a problem to be solved.' He began to pace up and down. Then he patted his shabby pockets. 'Damn!' he said. 'I have mislaid my pipe in the *fracas*. I know I had it with me. It must be on the floor. You two look for it while I think.'

We searched and he pondered.

'We have to attract Lady M – 's attention without alarming her,' he said. 'We must also remember that the stranger we followed into the house may have come for reasons other than to engage the domestic staff in sexual intercourse. He may well be an emissary from the blackmailer. If so he could well still be on the premises, and one or more of the servants may be in league with him. We must be careful.'

'There is a maid's uniform hanging in one of the closets we passed,' said Megan. 'I could slip it on and go upstairs in search of her Ladyship. My appearance would not startle her and I could pass on a message to her.'

'A capital suggestion,' said Holmes. 'I will wait here, and Scott, you must resume your station in the street.'

'If you two gentlemen could help me get undressed and dressed again, it will speed things up,' said Megan.

'That would seem a task best suited to Mr Scott's talents,' said Holmes. 'Ah! My pipe!' He picked it up from a corner of the room where it had lain unnoticed. 'This will aid the thought processes.'

Megan sent me off to fetch the uniform from the closet we had passed earlier while she began to strip off her rather grubby woollen dress.

'A wash is called for,' said Holmes. 'You are rather dirty.'

'Comes of fucking in a coal hole,' she said, looking at herself. 'A quick all-over sluice will do. There is a sink over there. If the young gentleman will wash the grime off his own hands, he can help me.'

I noticed that she was shivering a little.

'No chance of some warm water, I suppose,' she said.

'No time,' said Holmes. 'Cold it will have to be.'

I washed myself, drying my hands and face on another sheet.

'Now,' she said. 'Give me a good splashing.' She was standing, almost naked in the middle of the floor.

'Your hat,' I reminded her.

'Silly me,' she said and raised her arms to take it off. Then she lifted her hair up and posed in front of me. In spite of the urgency of the moment, I could not help but notice how enticing she looked even though she was streaked with coal

141

dust. Mr Pego reacted and stood hungrily up. She of course spotted what was happening at once.

'Another fuck?' she said, licking her lips in a most provoking manner.

'Not now!' said Holmes sternly.

Picking up a large dishcloth, I began to wipe her down. At the touch of the cold, damp rag, she gave out a little squeal. As her bare titties shook, my virile member thrust out once more. Holmes noticed.

'I can see that I will have to attend to the young lady's ablutions,' he said. 'Get her domestic's uniform ready.'

As Megan, still shivering but well aware of the effect she was having on me, twisted first one way and then the other while Holmes plied the cloth, I meanwhile tried to regain my critical faculties.

'I think your young gentleman could do with a splash of cold water, too,' said Megan.

'That is up to him,' said Holmes, gruffly. 'Now, that will do. Where's the dress?'

I stepped forward and slipped it down over her head, although not without a twinge of disappointment as its voluminous folds hid her thin body from sight. Holmes stepped back to inspect the effect.

'That won't do at all,' he said. 'Far too large. Fetch a smaller uniform.'

'There's only one in there,' I said.

'Damn!' he said. 'We simply can't send her up into the house like this. She looks more like an entrant in some village sack race. Anyone will notice in an instant.'

'What shall we do?' I asked.

'I shall think,' said Holmes, puffing once more on his pipe.

'If you please, Sir?' said Megan. 'I have an idea.'

'Don't interrupt,' I said. 'Mr Holmes is thinking.'

'Don't be rude!' she said. She turned to Holmes. 'The young gentleman is the nearest in size. He can put the dress on.'

'Certainly not!' I said. 'I shall do no such thing.' I waited, confident that Holmes would come up with a more suitable scheme.

'That is not a bad idea,' said Holmes to my horror. 'He only has to escape the close attention of the rest of the household and make his way up to the drawing room. As long as Lady M— is alone, he should be able to creep quietly in and make himself known to her without causing her any great alarm.'

'But, but,' I stuttered, feeling that events were slipping beyond my control.

'Be quick,' said Holmes. 'Help him into the dress,' he said to Megan. 'But you'll have to get rid of his own clothing first.'

Megan wriggled out of the over-large garment and, naked once more, began to undress me. I surrendered to my fate. Once again Mr Pego rose up so that she had some difficulty in pulling my trousers down over his aroused projection. Quickly she took my balls in one hand and gave a sharp squeeze. I squealed with the pain and as Mr Pego drooped for a moment, she had me trouserless before her. I drew in a deep breath and as I tried to regain my composure, she dropped the dress down over my head, pulling the skirts right down and smoothing it into place.

'That's it,' she said with a mocking look. 'A much better fit. Now, turn round and I'll do up the back.'

I obeyed, still preoccupied with the ache in my balls. She busied herself with the fastenings and when all was to her satisfaction, stepped back to inspect her handiwork.

'He needs a cap,' she said. 'There must be one in the cupboard to go with the dress.'

A cap was found and placed on my head.

'What do you think, Sir?' she said to Holmes.

'He'll pass muster,' he said. 'Anyway we really have no other option. At least his shoes are hidden. Now,' he said to me, 'remember to take short steps and maintain a posture of deference. Take a turn about the room while I have a look at you.'

'Let me get into my own dress again,' Megan said, 'And we'll coach him.'

I tried to walk like a woman.

'Not very good,' said Holmes. 'You'll never make a

143

detective if you cannot master the arts of disguise. Why I remember I once had to play the part of a nursemaid for several days while solving the Case of the Kidnapped Heiress. I flatter myself that I became remarkably adept at the changing and bathing of infants, although it is not an experience I would choose to repeat. At least you only have to pass as a maid for a short while.'

I struggled manfully to perfect my impersonation.

'That will have to do,' said Holmes impatiently. 'Just try to keep out of sight until you find Lady M − .'

'Off you go,' said Megan, patting me on the bottom. 'And try not to clump as you walk.'

And so I was sent out on my errand.

As I crept towards the servants stairs, I took stock of the situation. Somewhere in the house were the two maids. Since they had fled without their uniforms, which were still in the laundry along with Holmes and Megan, they would be immediately pre-occupied with finding some alternative clothing. Also possibly in the house was the well-dressed stranger, although if he were simply in the habit of calling at the house in order to fuck the maids he had doubtless slipped out again into the evening. If on the other hand he was indeed the blackmailer's emissary, he would have sought out Lady M − in order to deliver his message. On balance, this was the more likely situation since Holmes had clearly worked out that some member of the household was in league with the blackmailer and was supplying details of who was entertained in the absence abroad of Lord M − . It was therefore safer to assume that the well-dressed man was part of the plot. I had to keep out of his sight. I had no knowledge of how many other staff might be kept apart from the two who had been surprised by Holmes. One could assume at least a cook, possibly a housekeeper, a lady's maid and a manservant. I had to take care.

I further recalled that the arrangement had been that a servant would make a signal from an upstairs window on behalf of Lady M − when the message arrived. Clearly Lady M − had one trusted confidante among her staff. Unless she had mistakenly relied on one of the two denuded maids in the basement, this was a certain argument for at least one further domestic somewhere in the house.

At the top of the stairs I looked round cautiously. All was clear. I moved into the hallway. There was no sound. At the front of the house were doors to the left and the right. One would be the drawing room in which I might hope to find Lady M —. I looked into the room on the right. It was a dining room and empty of people although a cold meal of substantial proportions was laid out on the side. I thought again.

The signs suggested that this was cook's night off. This would account for the cold cuts that had been left. At least that was one less unwelcome surprise in waiting. However the quantity of food made it plain that guests were expected. I would have to hurry. I looked into the other room. The drawing room. Then I breathed a sigh of relief. Over by the window was Lady M —. She was alone, looking thoughtfully out into the street.

I entered and coughed. Lady M — turned round.

'What is it — ' she began. Then she looked more closely at me and started back.

'Who are you?' she said imperiously. 'Where is Esther?'

'Don't be alarmed, Lady M —' I said. 'It is I, Andrew Scott, Mr Holmes' assistant.'

'Good God!' she said. 'You gave me a terrible start. Why on earth are you dressed like that?'

I began to explain as well as I could. However I was barely halfway through the story when to my horror a door at the far end of the room opened and there stood the well-dressed stranger. 'Ah, Dear Lady,' he said, addressing himself to Lady M —. 'I think I have found the papers that your husband asked me to collect, so my business is completed.'

He looked in my direction. Luckily he seemed not to notice anything untoward about my appearance. Then he looked back towards Lady M —, plainly waiting for her to react to his statement.

'Ah, er, Hetty,' she said to me, at the same time screwing up her face and generally making it clear to me that I would have to act out my part for the moment. 'Hetty, would you serve drinks?' Then she walked over to me and said in a low voice, 'I've no idea what is going on. The butler's pantry is at the foot of the stairs. You will have to carry out Esther's duties.'

Downstairs, no-one was to be seen and there was no time to go looking for Holmes and Megan and find out what they were doing. I returned with glasses and a decanter of what looked like sherry. Lady M — was in deep conversation with the stranger.

'Put them down over there, Hetty,' she said.

I did as I was bid and withdrew. I must own to the fact that I was becoming considerably hot and bothered. As I stood in the hall wondering what to do next, to my alarm there was a ring at the front door.

'Answer it will you, Hetty,' Lady M — called out. 'John has the evening off and Esther is busy upstairs.' At least she had managed to pass on much-needed information about the disposition of the other members of the household. Nonetheless I had been placed in the awkward position of having to cope with whoever was on the steps outside. With lowered eyes and ready to bob demurely, I opened the front door.

Two women stood there, dressed in the height of fashion. 'The Honourable Gwendolen Fairfax and Miss Cecily Cardew,' said a familiar voice. 'Lady M — is expecting us.'

I leaped backwards in surprise. Gwendolen and Cecily! Two of my dearest and most intimate friends (*see Oyster 3*).

'What is it, girl?' said Cecily sharply. 'You look as though you've seen a ghost.'

'It's Andrew,' I hissed, knowing that I could not escape recognition and hoping to get the surprise over with there and then without any exclamations that would draw attention to us. 'It's me — ' Unfortunately I was so overcome by the surprise of our encounter that I choked and began to cough.

'What!' said Gwendolen. Then she looked at me carefully. Her eyes widened with amazement.

'It can't be! Stop coughing and stand up straight so we can get a good look at you.'

My eyes streaming, I spluttered, 'It is, but for Heaven's Sake, keep your voices down.'

'Well, it could be him,' murmured Cecily sweetly to her companion. 'But it's hard to tell in this light and him dressed up like that.'

In desperation, knowing that I had only seconds to make the situation clear to them, I recalled the one thing that was most likely to convince them that I was in fact Andrew. Abruptly I pulled up my dress. Underneath, of course, I had nothing on. Like a faithful hound responding to its master, my cock leaped into sight. Cecily and Gwendolen both let out simultaneous cries of recognition.

'It is him,' said Cecily. 'I'd recognise that Thing anywhere.'

'True, Cecily,' said Gwendolen. She looked carefully at me. 'I did not know that you numbered dressing up in women's clothes among your interests.' She walked up to me, took my engorged prick in her hand and looked back at Cecily. 'Who could overlook something like that,' she said. She began to rub her hand up and down the charged length of my member. 'And to think that we believed we were invited for a quiet meal with our friend Priscilla. Mind you,' she went on to Cecily, 'she has always been fond of contriving unusual entertainment for her friends. This promises to be an excellent evening as long as Andrew is not the only man present. Maybe they are all to be attired in this way.'

'No! It's not like that at all,' I whispered urgently. Quickly I gave the two of them a brief description of the events that had transpired. All the while Gwendolen was playing most teasingly with my prick so that I had great difficulty in keeping my mind on my tale.

'Hetty! Show my guests in,' came Lady M—'s voice.

Pulling myself together, I disentangled myself from Gwendolen's grip, tugged my dress down, and adjusted my maid's cap. 'Not a word in front of the stranger,' I managed to hiss. 'I suspect that he is part of another plot altogether.'

I ushered them into the drawing room and closed the door behind them. Outside I took a deep breath and tried once more to think. The situation was that Lady M— knew that I was Andrew Scott, assistant to Porlock Holmes, the Great Detective. Cecily and Gwendolen also knew that I was

Andrew Scott but did not know that Lady M— was privy to this information. And *vice versa*. The well-dressed stranger, as far as he had noticed me, thought that I was Hetty the maid. Neither Lady M—, Gwendolen nor Cecily had more than a sketchy idea of the events that had brought me to this state of frantic impersonation. I needed help in order to decide what to do next. It would have to be Holmes.

I picked my way carefully down the servants' stairs once more, hoping that I would stumble upon my friends rather than the two scullery maids. The laundry room would be the place to start. I minced towards it.

'Sixpence for a fuck,' said a quiet voice behind me.

I nearly jumped out of my skin. Megan! Then I let out a yelp of surprise as an intruding finger was shoved forcefully between the cheeks of my bum, probing through the thin material of my dress. As I turned, she turned with me, nipping me sharply in the nape of my neck with her teeth.

'Not now!' I said, reaching behind me to fend her off. Suddenly a door opened.

'Who are you?' said a new voice. Someone who was clearly a *bone fide* ladies' maid was looking at the two of us.

'You must be Lady M—'s personal maid,' came a further voice. Holmes had emerged from the laundry. 'Don't worry, my dear,' he said. 'I can explain everything. We are all friends of your mistress.'

The newcomer looked as though she was about to bolt in confusion and fright.

'We must keep our voices down,' said Holmes. 'Are you indeed Esther?'

'Yes — ' she said reluctantly, still poised like a nervous gazelle, ready for flight.

'I know from Lady M— that you can be trusted. You have been commissioned to pass on a message from the window to a crossing sweeper in the event of some unwelcome visitor to the house. I am that crossing sweeper and this,' he pointed at me, 'is my assistant.'

'Dr Motson, I presume,' said the maid Esther, relief spreading over her face.

'Scott, actually,' I said. 'Dr Motson is on holiday.'

Holmes took her, still trembling, by the arm and led her into the laundry. Megan and I followed. Rapidly he explained the situation as far as he knew it. When he had finished, I in turn brought him up-to-date with the events upstairs. It remained only to ascertain the whereabouts of the two naked domestics who had been so heartily engaged in sexual congress with the stranger before our arrival upon the scene.

'They are locked in a store cupboard,' volunteered Megan. 'They were hiding inside and I turned the key on them. The stranger must have told them to keep out of the way. They still do not have any clothes.'

Esther, by now more or less calmed, offered her services in furthering our endeavours. 'Her Ladyship's guests are expecting supper,' she said. 'But I do not know if the strange gentleman is also to eat with them. I have to wait on them.'

'And Mr Scott, also,' said Holmes.

'Noooo!' I howled. 'I can't do that!'

'Yes you can and will,' said Holmes firmly. 'As long as you do not arouse the suspicion of the stranger, you will be quite safe. Everyone else knows of your imposture, if not the whole story that accounts for it, so none of them will give you away in front of him. But I need you to be there to observe what happens and to get a message to Lady M—'

'What is that?' I asked.

'She must be reassured that I am on call below stairs. I also need to know whether she understands that we need confirmation that the stranger is indeed part of the conspiracy with her husband.'

At that moment a bell jangled.

'That will be Her Ladyship,' said Esther. 'If Mr Scott, or Hetty, will accompany me, we must serve supper.'

Before I could protest any further, I was shoved up the stairs behind her by Holmes and Megan.

My first venture into domestic service was growing more fraught by the minute. It was not an easy meal. The stranger had indeed stayed for dinner. By dint of great concentration, I managed to perform my duties with a degree of verisimilitude, coached and watched over as I was by Esther the maid. However I had reckoned without the unfortunate sense of humour of Cecily. I was standing dutifully at Lady M — 's shoulder while she helped herself to a plateful of soup when I felt a hand slide under the hem of my dress, run rapidly up my thighs and begin to insinuate itself between them. Instinctively I clenched my buttocks but too late. A delicate hand cupped my balls and began to squeeze them rhythmically.

I lurched forward, slopping the soup into Lady M — 's lap. She shot backwards in her chair, just managing to avoid the deluge but bumping into me as she did so. The soup ladle dropped to the floor and I hastily banged the tureen on to the table before ducking down on hands and knees to retrieve it. My testicles were released but the same hand flipped my skirt over my bum. The strange man was seated on the other side of the table so that at least I was concealed from his gaze. As I groped around for the ladle, I was assaulted in a most outrageous fashion from left and right as Lady M — joined in the sport. I felt a stinging pinch to the cheek.

'Do be careful, Hetty,' said Lady M — . 'You have nearly spoilt my dress. Help her up, Esther.'

Flustered and humiliated, I scrambled up.

'Fetch a cloth and mop up this mess,' Lady M — continued, before turning back to the strange man and resuming her polite dinner table chit chat. I retrieved the tureen, found another ladle and, struggling to regain some composure, went round to serve the stranger.

To my horror, as I bent over him, he also patted me on the bum. Of course I had to submit to his coarse advances without flinching. Such is ever the lot of the servant, I remembered as he managed to press himself against me with impudent familiarity.

By now I realised that I was likely to be grabbed and fondled every time I approached the table. Only Gwendolen had so far kept her hands off me, but I knew her too well to regard her as trustworthy. Esther, bless her, did her best to keep me out of harm's way. Somehow the meal was served and eaten. As it wore on, I became considerably adept at avoiding any surreptitious strokings and intrusions into my private parts.

Then, just as we were serving the dessert, the stranger asked to be excused for a moment. Esther directed him down the hallway to the cloakroom and at last I could speak my mind.

'That was most unfair,' I said, coming up to the table. 'You very nearly gave the game away.'

'I am sorry,' said Cecily contritely. Then she whipped up my skirt from the front and her sister pushed me rudely forward. My prick slapped down on the table, landing on the edge of a plate. Before I had the time to whisk it away under cover again, Gwendolen trapped it with her hand.

'What an interesting object to see served up to one,' she said to Lady M —. 'What a pity that we cannot have one each.'

'We shall have to sample it in turns,' said her hostess.

I tried to pull myself free.

'Lady M —' I said desperately, 'I have an urgent communication from Mr Holmes.'

'Of course,' she said, 'I had quite forgotten. There is another prick downstairs. As soon as we have bidden Mr Pride goodnight, we can bring him up from below.'

'Lady M —' I said, 'Mr Holmes suspects that your visitor is in league with the blackmailer. Has he attempted to pass on any message from the scoundrel?'

'Yes,' said Lady M —, 'but there is no time to explain further. He will be coming back in a minute. Let him go,' she continued to Gwendolen and Cecily. 'We can resume our entertainment in a little while.' I was released. Mr Pego, who in spite of my confusion had shown every sign of wanting to come out and take part in the engagement, was hidden once more from sight. Esther took over the task of bringing coffee and I made my escape once more below stairs.

A muffled thudding was coming from the cupboard where the two maids were imprisoned. Then I heard the sound of a struggle. I dashed into the laundry fearing the worst. Holmes was helpless on his back in a large wickerwork basket, trying to get up again. However Megan had him pinned down, her legs on each side of his waist and was fairly bouncing up and down on him.

151

'Get this woman off me!' he cried out as he saw me. 'I have an injured back.'

I stooped forward to pull her off but she instantly reached under my dress and once more Mr Pego was hauled out into full view.

'What a sorry looking fellow,' she said. 'I must lick it into shape.'

I realised that she was thoroughly enthroned on Holmes and thus securely seated, she proceeded to bend forward and take me in her mouth. With the expertise of her profession, she all but swallowed my member while her tongue cradled its underside. Clasping me tightly round the backs of my thighs, she began to suck and lap me into such a state of excitement that I became quite incapable of any further resistance.

Soon, as she lifted herself up and down on the still protesting Holmes, I began to respond, thrusting in and out of her eager mouth. Yet, ever mindful of my errand, I attempted at the same time to inform Holmes of what Lady M— had said concerning her visitor.

'I knew he was a wrong 'un,' he said, beginning in spite of himself to enter into the spirit of the occasion. His eyes closed and he frowned with concentration even as he started to pant with his efforts.

'One of us must follow him when he leaves,' he gasped.

'I think,' I panted, 'that it had better be you. I have to attend to the two young ladies upstairs.'

'Who are they?' he asked breathlessly.

'It's a long story but I know them both,' I said. Then I felt the first stirrings from my swollen balls as the beginnings of my cum began to spurt along my cock. Megan sucked hungrily at me and I began to discharge myself into her warm, wet mouth. Thirstily she swallowed my copious bounty while still levering herself up and down on Holmes like one possessed.

'If I ever get out of here and am still able to walk,' he said, 'I shall attempt the task. But first, I'd better get on with my immediate duties, or your Welsh friend will never let me go.'

I realised that in spite of his verbal reluctance he also had been provoked to his coming. Fairly snorting with his efforts, he was matching Megan stroke for stroke. For a man of such cerebral habits he was proving surprisingly athletic, although I recalled that he was used to long moorland excursions according to Mrs P – 's account.

By now I was becoming quite drained with the activities of the day. A last jet of cum trickled rather than gushed down Megan's throat and she began to lick me clean. My prick slipped from her mouth and a final milky dribble fell on Holmes. Luckily he failed to notice its descent as he also was completing his spending. Satisfied at last, Megan ceased her writhing and let him slip free as well.

'That should be sevenpence each,' she said. 'But since we had not come to any agreement beforehand, I shall have to rely on your generosity.'

'Now, Madam, will you please release me,' said Holmes, 'or our quarry will escape.'

Megan lifted herself up. 'All sweaty , I am,' she said. 'I need another wash.'

'Well, you stay down here and clean yourself up,' I said. 'I have to get back to the dining room at once.'

Once more pulling my dress down, I looked about me.

'Your cap is all awry,' she said. 'Here, let me straighten it.'

'Give me a hand with Mr Holmes, first,' I said. 'He seems to be stuck in the basket.' Together we took him by the arms and hauled him to his feet. As we let him go, he clutched his back and winced.

'An old campaign injury,' he said. 'South Africa.' For a moment he stood, bent double and then took a deep breath and drew himself up. 'My pipe. It's gone again.' Megan fussed round him like a mother hen, tucking his shirt into his trousers, before retrieving his pipe and other belongings.

'I shall go outside and wait in the street,' he said. 'When you have finished your duties upstairs, you must make your way round to my rooms. If I have not returned, Mrs Sayers will look after you. Now, I must be gone.' So saying he let himself out into the darkness.

'What are you going to do?' I asked Megan. 'I don't think you should linger. Remember that there are two maids, in all

153

probability still naked, locked in the cupboard. It would never do if they managed to get out and found you here. One at least is implicated in the plot.'

'Don't worry yourself about me,' she said. 'I promise to avoid detection.' There was no point in interrogating her further on her intentions. I would have to trust to her common sense. Then a thought struck me.

'Where are my clothes?' I said. 'I shall have to change back out of this dress before I leave.'

'Oh, you don't want to bother with those raggedy old things,' she said. 'You look very fetching as you are.'

'But where are they?' I insisted.

'In the corner over there. You get upstairs and I'll fish them out and leave them where you can find them later.' Once again I was propelled back into the fray.

At the top of the stairs I stumbled. The fatigue of the day was beginning to affect me. As I entered the dining room, Lady M— looked up.

'Back again so soon, Hetty?' she said.

'I would prefer to be called by my correct name,' I said.

'Not dressed like that,' she said, tweaking provocatively at the hem of my dress. 'Cecily and Gwendolen have been telling me all about your artistic interests (*see Oyster 3*). But where is Mr Holmes? I think it is time he was brought up from below stairs so we can have a council of war and then possibly some entertainment.'

'He has resumed his watch in the street,' I said. 'Your gentleman caller has to be followed when he leaves.'

'That should be in a minute or two,' she said. 'Esther is seeing him out.'

'He brought some message from the blackmailer, I presume,' I said.

'A demand that I hand over a letter signing away much of my fortune. I told him that I would have to see my attorney. The letters of assignment have to be prepared within two days. He will call again to collect them.'

'I am certain that Mr Holmes will be able to apprehend the principal in this diabolic scheme.'

'Then there is nothing more that we can do for the

moment,' she said. 'Cecily has a plan to take our minds off this sorry affair.'

The splendidly full-bosomed Cecily stood up. I realised that the back of her dress was already unbuttoned.

'Since Esther is otherwise engaged for the moment, you must play the part of ladies' maid. There are a couple of fastenings that I cannot easily reach.' She presented her back to me. Already her creamy shoulders and back were partly exposed. Fumbling slightly, I undid the remaining restraints on her freedom. Under instruction, I pushed her dress and chemise off her shoulders. Her splendidly lush titties sprang into view.

'Your hands,' she said. Obediently I reached round her from behind. She took my hands and placed them firmly on her breasts. They were warm and plump in my palms.

'A little attention to my nipples, I think,' she said. My fingers closed over her already protruding nipples. I felt them harden under my touch.

'Squeeze them,' Cecily said. I began to rub and fondle her. All fatigue was forgotten as I felt her respond to me.

'A little harder,' she said. 'Oh! That feels so lovely.' Nestling her bum against Mr Pego, she started to twist and sway, forcing her titties into the palms of my hands. As I began to stroke her, she was breathing more and more heavily.

'Keep going!' she gasped. 'A bit harder. Don't be afraid of hurting me. I am quite impervious to pain when my breasts are being massaged. Oh! Lady M – ' she said to our hostess, 'Is it not simply the most delightful experience to feel a man's hands on one's bosom?'

I looked over in Lady M – 's direction. She had flung herself down in an upholstered chair and I noticed that one hand had crept under her skirt and she was beginning to frig herself into a state of excitement.

'Gwendolen, please,' she said. 'Hetty has got her hands full. I wonder if you could be of assistance.'

Gwendolen, ever the courteous guest, rose and knelt down in front of her. Carefully she drew Lady M – 's skirt up. She responded by leaning back and parting her thighs. I saw the forest of her quim spread out before me. As though unveiling some rare treasure to an expectant audience, Gwendolen slipped one finger under her and felt for a moment. Lady M – gave a shudder of pleasure as the finger disappeared into her. Then it was slowly drawn upwards. A second finger joined it in its unseen cave, then her lips were carefully parted and Lady M – 's cunney was opened out to the public gaze. Instinctively I clutched Cecily harder and began to rub my hands up and down her glorious breasts. My prick jutted out, pressing into her. Cecily lifted up both her skirts and mine and as the embroidered material rubbed against the very tip of my distended member, I was brought to a state of almost uncomfortable readiness. I felt her cheeks part and she reached down, taking hold of the end of my prick and guiding it easily into her. Once I was properly seated, she stopped all movement, and paused expectantly.

As though recognising her cue, Gwendolen began to rub her fingers up and down in Lady M – 's cunney. She slipped still further down in her chair and spread herself wide. She let out a sudden cry of pleasure and I realised that Gwendolen's assiduous fingers had encountered Lady M – 's clit. As the slow but regular movements of her rubbing and caressing continued, I found myself automatically rubbing Cecily's nipples in a similar circular fashion. She was now bumping her cheeks against me, forcing me still deeper into her. Then she started to slip backwards and forwards on me, bending down so that I could thrust my entire member into her wet and welcoming tunnel.

Still watching the lovely display facing me, I kept time with Gwendolen's efforts. Lady M – began to turn her head from side to side, her mouth open and her eyes closed. She was moaning and quite oblivious to the rest of the world. I was banging and thrusting against Cecily like a man possessed. My knees were beginning to tremble with my exertions but so enervated was I from my day's repeated sexual exploits that although Mr Pego was in an almost painful state of excitement, there was no sign of that relieving gush that would mark the culmination of my efforts.

'More! More!' Cecily cried out, continuing to buck and

writhe on my impaling instrument. Gamely, I drove on, my balls smacking against her widespread thighs. In and out I thrust. Then, over-vigorous in my motion, my prick slipped out of her. Hungrily, she seized hold of it and almost rammed it up inside her again. Then as Lady M— began to cry out loud, Cecily also increased her pace to a frenzy. I sensed a final hot flush of ecstasy inside her and she and Lady M— came together, their near-delirious pleasure cries mingling.

Although my prick was wet and slippery with Cecily's copious juices, there was a hollow dryness within and a dull ache in my balls. Desperately I drove like a piston into her. She was in the full flow of her coming and her own juices were trickling down her thighs. She gave one last gasp and staggered. In my determination I had forced my whole weight on her. Weak from my efforts, I buckled at the knees and in an instant we had fallen forward onto the carpet. I lay on top of her, sapped of all energy as if I had also come. Yet my undischarged member remained obstinately and adamantly erect. Cecily slipped off me once more and we both fell over, she on her back with her legs raised, her hands rubbing and pressing against her bush, savouring the last moments of her spending.

I for my part was also flat on my back, my dress rucked up somewhere around my armpits and my prick bolt upright like a flagstaff. Dimly I realised that Esther the maid had entered the room. Obviously she was used to such scenes in the house for when Lady M— said 'The fanny fan!' to her, she immediately picked up some sort of Spanish lace fan from where it lay, obviously in readiness, on a shelf and began to waft it vigorously in front of her mistress's bared quim.

Gwendolen, her own needs as yet unattended to, was nonetheless looking quite happy, sitting back on her heels beside Lady M— and sucking the fingers that had just been so busily and skilfully engaged in their stimulating work.

'Our guest has gone?' asked Lady M—.

'Yes, Ma'am,' Esther answered, still fanning away.

'Good,' said Lady M—, continuing to expose herself to Esther's cooling mission. 'We must hope that Mr Holmes is successful in tracking him to his lair.' She glanced over to me.

157

'Gracious,' she said. 'You look as though you could do with some help.'

'May I rest here for a little while, Lady M — ' I said feebly. 'I fear I am quite worn out with events.'

'Of course,' she said understandingly. 'But there is Gwendolen to think of. I would like to think that you can satisfy her in due course.'

'I will try,' I said. 'Please do not take offence. I should like nothing better than to help her. I will do what I can as soon as possible.'

'Don't worry,' said Gwendolen. 'I have an idea. Don't move.'

As I gazed up at the ceiling, I became aware of a rustle of clothing. Suddenly everything went black. Gwendolen had lowered her quim onto my face!

For a moment I thought I would faint from lack of air as darkness enveloped me. Then she lifted herself up a fraction and I took a deep breath, drawing in the scent of her eager pussey while her dense hair filled my mouth and nostrils.

'Don't smother him,' came a voice, seemingly from far away. 'Esther, can you put a cushion behind his head. He needs to be lifted up a bit.' Lady M — was issuing orders like an experienced mistress of ceremonies. 'Gwendolen, if you lean forward you should be able to take him in your mouth.'

I felt warm lips nuzzling at the end of my prick. As her bum was raised, I could see once more. My head was carefully propped up. 'Be gentle with him,' ordered Lady M — . 'He must have had a hard day. Andrew, if you could just use your tongue on Gwendolen, I am certain she will be more than grateful.'

Gallantly I began to lick and tease at Gwendolen's cunney. Such was our position that I could not enter into her properly but I managed to rub against her delicately parted lips.

'That's lovely,' she said sympathetically. 'It's all I want for the moment. Just a lick and a promise.' Then she bent down and dabbed lightly at the very tip of my prick. Now at last I felt a quick contraction in my sorely tried balls. From deep inside me a small rivulet of cum pulsed up my prick. Just as it reached the top, Gwendolen withdrew. A rather feeble fountain shot up into the air.

'Poor thing,' said Cecily. 'A spent force. I suspect that that is all he has to offer for the time being. We must let him recover.'

I carried on tonguing Gwendolen as best I could. Delicious though the sensation was, I was near exhaustion, as well as thoroughly mortified that I had not been able to satisfy her. As waves of fatigue coursed through me, I was dimly aware that she had lifted herself from me.

'Fucked dry,' said a voice. 'Gwendolen, come over here and let us complete what he has started.' All went blank and I lapsed into near unconsciousness.

Coming as though from a great distance, I heard the murmur of voices. I was half aware of a door opening and closing. Time passed. More voices and the sound of low, earnest conversation seeped into my fatigue-dulled brain. I turned over on my side as though I were in bed.

'How unfortunate,' I heard someone say. 'He has been taxed beyond human endurance.'

'Unfortunate, indeed!' came a scornful voice. 'Look what he's doing! The dirty beast is playing with himself!'

Coming to with a start I realised that my hands had sought out the warmth and comfort of my prick and I was clasping it between them. Other hands turned me over on to my back once more.

'Don't be so harsh, Cecily,' said a more concerned voice. 'Look at his Thing. I've never seen it like that before. I much prefer it in its more usual state. I only hope it gets better soon.'

'If I might offer my advice Ma'am,' said a soft Welsh voice, 'We should let him lie for a few minutes more. If nothing happens then, I have a trick or two up my sleeve. It is a problem that I have often encountered in my trade.' Megan had been brought into the room.

Bewildered, I tried to sit up. 'What's happening?' I said.

'Nothing,' said Lady M — . 'That's the problem.'

My stomach rumbled.

'Too much fucking on an empty stomach,' said

Gwendolen. 'We must give him something to restore him to life.'

A bowl of by now cold soup was thrust under my chin. Then I was lifted into a sitting position while Gwendolen plied me with several spoonfulls. I swallowed obediently but as my strength returned, so did a feeling of mortification. I was being nursed like an invalid or worse still, a baby. I pushed the spoon away.

'I am quite capable of feeding myself,' I said crossly.

'Well, I suppose that's some improvement,' said Cecily. 'But I am being altogether too severe on you,' she continued, a note of contrition creeping into her voice. 'Maybe there's something more that can be done.'

At that, she lowered her still naked breasts so that they brushed against my dormant member. She began to swing them back and forth. Lady M — and Gwendolen crowded in on me, first one and then the other lowering themselves onto the carpet so that they could carry out a close inspection of Cecily's efforts.

'Nothing happening so far,' said Lady M —.

'I know it will work,' said Cecily. 'My great aunt was a nurse in the Crimea under Florence Nightingale. She said that she often did this to restore some unfortunate injured soldier to life. Indeed most of the nurses did. Of course they had to wait until the Lady with the Lamp had returned to her quarters.' As she talked, she continued her healing ministrations.

'Look! Something's happening now,' said Gwendolen. 'I saw a distinct sign of life.' Sure enough, Cecily's gentle persistence was bearing fruit. Mr Pego stirred and straightened. Struggling against the Law of Gravity, he began to raise himself up, inch by inch.

'*Penis redivivus*,' said Lady M — displaying an unexpected acquaintance with the language of the Classics.

'Like Excalibur emerging from the Lake,' said Gwendolen, not to be outdone in this display of learning.

'Not yet,' said Megan, practically. 'There's still a bend in it.'

'Some extra help is needed,' said Lady M —. Pressing her face close to my valiantly straining member, she began to lick carefully both at its tip and at Cecily's swollen nipples. Gwendolen joined in. Under their combined care, Mr Pego's revival continued.

'Now we must get him completely upright,' said Megan. 'He still needs some more time before he is completely ready to enter into any further activity.' I was hauled to my feet and released. As my dress dropped into position, I stood there, my legs apart, trying to steady myself.

'Fetch a chair,' said Lady M— and as Esther hurried forward with an upright, I sank gratefully down, my knees almost giving way once more.

'At least we can bring him up to date with what has been occurring,' said Lady M—.

I listened, glad that for the moment there were no further calls upon my energies. It transpired that the stranger had left the house and that Esther had managed to dash upstairs and give the pre-arranged signal from the window. She had caught sight of Holmes waiting up the street under a gas lamp. The stranger had walked off down the road and had then hailed a passing cab. Esther was sure that Holmes had set off after him. I remembered that Holmes had had his own cab waiting round the corner for just such an eventuality. I also recalled that I was under orders to return to his Marylebone Road rooms and report what had gone on in the house. I explained what had to be done to Lady M— and the others.

'First I must find my clothes,' I said. 'Megan, you were going to have them ready for me.'

'They're very dirty,' she said. 'And there is still the problem of the two incarcerated maids.'

'Esther, you must go down and release them at once. Bring them up here. I must have a severe word with them. One at least is betraying my confidences. We must find out which is the guilty party and she must leave immediately.'

'If it please you, Ma'am,' said Esther, 'I don't think that it is Olive. She's fresh from the country and none too bright, but I don't think there's an ounce of malice in her. She's just very fond of fucking.'

'Very well,' said Lady M—. 'I shall have to question them one by one.'

'But if you will forgive me,' I said. 'I must return to Mr Holmes' rooms as soon as possible.'

'You'll have to go like that,' said Lady M —. 'We can send your sweeper's rags round in the morning.'

'Is that wise, Ma'am,' said Megan. 'Dressed like that, he will have to make the entire journey on foot. If he gets a cab he will surely betray himself by his voice, if nothing else.'

'You're right,' said Lady M —. She paused, deep in thought. 'I know, someone must go with him. You can take my carriage. Send for James.'

'Lady M —,' said Cecily, 'may I suggest that Gwendolen and myself go with him? He is not yet fully restored to health.'

'On second thoughts, we will all accompany him,' said Lady M —. 'The problem of the maids can be dealt with tomorrow. Esther, let them out but make sure neither of them leaves the house.'

So all of us, Megan included in the party at Lady M —'s insistence, crowded into her carriage and set off through the night to beard Holmes in his den.

Of the journey, I can remember little. I was still considerably fatigued and such was the warmth engendered by our densely packed confinement that I dozed throughout, lulled by the motion of our passage. I was aware of low conversation and the occasional squeal of pleasure but all was subdued and relaxed.

Some while later the carriage drew to a halt and I came to.

'We have arrived at Mr Holmes' place,' said Lady M — and we all piled out and swarmed up the front steps.

'Good Gracious!' came Mrs Sayers' voice. '*Five* ladies come to call and at such a late hour. However I am afraid that Mr Holmes is not at home, nor is his assistant, Mr Scott. They went out much earlier and neither has been seen since.' She peered at us more closely. 'Lady M —!' she said. 'If it is in connection with the case that he is working on, I can only suggest that you come in and wait for him. I am sure that one or other of them will return soon.'

I realised that dressed as I was she had not recognised me, but before I could make my identity known to her, Lady M — swept in and we were all ushered upstairs to Holmes' study. Mrs Sayers poked the fire into life and then bustled out with the promise of a pot of coffee to come. We settled down to wait.

'What shall we do to pass the time?' said Cecily. Several glances were turned in my direction. 'Andrew, we need entertainment. There must be some parlour game that you can suggest.'

'I would like first of all to change back into some of my own clothes, if I might be excused for a short while.'

'Certainly not,' said Lady M — . 'We've grown used to you in that rather fetching outfit. It suits you.'

I opened my mouth to protest at being so bullied and ordered about but then remembered that Lady M — had engaged Holmes to act on her behalf and, while I had no idea of the financial arrangements involved, it seemed to me in all probability that I was under some quasi-contractual obligation to do as she said. More to the point, I knew that she was under some considerable strain from the whole affair and that it would be kind to humour her. Holmes in any case would not be best pleased if I managed to upset his client over what I suspected he would feel was a trivial matter.

I accepted that for the time being I would have to remain in women's clothing, and that my more pressing worry was that I should not be able to take any part demanded of me in any game suggested by those present. I would have to offer an alternative proposition.

'A game of whist?' I suggested. 'There are cards in the bureau.'

'Too boring,' said Lady M — .

'Bezique?' I tried.

'You'll have to do better than that,' she said.

'I'd like to fuck,' said Gwendolen. I must have looked alarmed because Megan, bless her, came to my rescue.

'I know a game that I learned from a gentleman friend in Portsmouth. We used to play it in his lodgings with his companions.' The other looked rather unimpressed. 'It really is great fun,' she went on brightly.

'It is not some intellectual pursuit, I hope,' said Gwendolen. 'It is not *intellectual* stimulation that I need.

'Fucking would be nice,' said Cecily.

'It is quite simple,' said Megan supportively, 'And it is probably the nearest thing to fucking that can be arranged until Mr Scott has gathered his strength.'

'Tell us about it,' said Lady M —.

'And while you do,' said Gwendolen, 'I have just had an idea. Look!' She had been busily rooting around in her bag as she spoke. Now she triumphantly drew out a familiar object.

'A dildo!' came a chorus of delighted recognition.

'But no ordinary dildo,' she said. She walked over to me, holding the object in her hand. Once more my dress was pulled up and Mr Pego put on display.

'See!' she said. 'Do you not see the similarity?'

'Not much,' said Lady M —. 'One is up and the other is down. If we are to make comparisons, they will both have to be in the same state.'

'Both up would be the more pleasing prospect,' said Cecily. 'In any case, we can hardly bend the delightful object that dear Gwendolen has procured for us. One of us must help Andrew in an attempt at re-erection.'

'I might manage it, if I may,' said Megan. 'My gentleman friend in the Navy often had such a problem when he had just returned from a long sea voyage.'

'By all means, go ahead,' said Lady M —. 'We will watch.'

'I need some butter,' said Megan. 'Perhaps we might ring for the housekeeper?'

'Mrs Sayers is of a rather puritan disposition,' I said. 'It would be better if any object that could cause offence were hidden from her.'

In truth, I had no idea whatsoever if there was any truth in what I said. Indeed I surmised that in her capacity as Holmes' housekeeper, she had long grown used to an array of odd happenings and strange habits. However I was quite determined not to be confronted by her in my present revealing state. In any case, she was of advancing years and since she had not so far recognised me, got up as I was, I did not want to cause her a fright.

'I accept your point,' said Lady M — . 'Let us present a united and decorous front.' So both dildo and member were put away and I moved over into a corner where the light did not catch me. Megan came and stood beside me while the others arranged themselves elegantly on a *chaise longue* and Holmes' leather bound armchair. Mrs Sayers was sent for and butter ordered.

'A tray of sandwiches, Your Ladyship?' asked Mrs Sayers, having no inkling of course as to the purpose for which the butter was needed.

'That would be nice,' said Cecily. 'But make sure there is plenty of butter on them.'

'Ham sandwiches?' asked Mrs Sayers. 'We have a large smoked ham, just delivered from the country at the behest of one of Mr Holmes' acquaintances.'

'That sounds splendid,' said Lady M — . 'With mustard.'

'But not *in* the sandwiches,' said Megan hastily, from her semi-obscurity. She had obviously foreseen the possibility of a painful problem as far as I was concerned, if, as I suspected, I had accurately divined the use to which the butter might be put.

The arrangements were made and we awaited her return. The others turned to talk of intimate encounters while I took the opportunity to sit down once more. Megan sat beside me, keeping a watchful eye and indeed hand on my recovery. Such was her closeness that I relaxed and began to hope that I should be able to regain my full faculties in the not too distant future. She gave my thigh a little squeeze.

'Don't look so worried,' she whispered. 'We'll soon have you up and about again.' Cecily and Gwendolen were entertaining Lady M — with stories of their schooldays in Somerset (*see Oyster 3*) when Mrs Sayers returned with a large salver of sandwiches, mustard in a pot and coffee. Putting it all down on an occasional table that I had earlier noticed because of its marquetry inlay depicting an Eastern scene of astonishing complexity and frankness, she retired. She volunteered the information that she was more than used to having to wait up all hours for Holmes, so we could safely leave any callers to her. The fire was stoked up once more and we were left to our own devices.

Hands reached out for the sandwiches, then Gwendolen paused. 'Megan has first call on them,' she said, 'or at least on the butter in them.'

With a well-mannered curtsy, Megan opened up one sandwich and inspected it. 'That'll do nicely,' she said. 'Just the thing to produce an inflexible friend. Lift your skirt up, Hetty!'

'Andrew, please!' I said.

'You're Hetty until I've dealt with you. Then maybe you'll be an Andrew again.' I stood up and hiked up my skirt. Megan extracted the ham from the sandwich, took a good bite out of it and then scraped a generous helping of butter into the palm of her hand. After she had rubbed it into a suitably soft state, she bent down and began anointing my prick. As she rubbed it into my rather wretched member with her gentle hands, I began to perk up a little. The others looked on with deep interest.

'Can't we speed things up a bit,' said Lady M— rather unhelpfully. 'A good dollop of mustard should produce some reaction.'

At such an idea, I flinched and wilted once more.

'Please, Ma'am,' said Megan. 'Now see what you've done.' Not knowing how Lady M— would take such a reprimand from one of the lower orders, I pursed my lips. Then I realised with a sense of relief that she had been teasing me all along. She burst out laughing.

'I'm sorry, Andrew,' she said. 'How we are mocking you. It is only in fun. Let me reassure you that whatever happens or does not happen tonight, I have every confidence that we can have a most delightful fuck in the near future.'

'And me,' said Gwendolen.

'Me, too,' said Cecily.

At this chorus of assent I relaxed, knowing I was truly among friends. In response to both my easier mood and Megan's renewed buttering, Mr Pego began to recover. There was a round of applause. Emboldened, I strode over to the centre of the room, flourishing my awakened manhood. Megan carefully stroked its underside and then withdrew her hand.

'I don't think you need propping up any further,' she said, standing back to admire her handiwork. There were nods of approval all round. Then Gwendolen delved into her bag and drew out the dildo again.

'Now,' she said, coming over and holding it parallel to my prick, 'What do you notice?'

'It's Andrew! To the life!' exclaimed Lady M — with delight. 'How on earth did you get hold of such a Thing?'

'It's a long story,' said Gwendolen, 'but it was given to me by a mutual friend when we were on a bicycling holiday in Northamptonshire (*see Oyster 4*). She is an artist and potter of considerable skill and persuaded him to model for it.'

'I should dearly like to have such a memento of him for my own entertainment,' said Lady M — . 'Are there more copies to be had?'

'I am certain that can be arranged,' said Gwendolen. 'But in the meantime, I realise that I have a further example of her craft.'

Another dildo was produced. At once I recognised it but the others looked most puzzled. Lady M — reached out to inspect it more closely. 'But, it's got *writing* on it,' she cried out. 'I can't quite make out what it says. This is a very strange Thing indeed.'

'It is a signature,' I said, holding it up to the light. 'Count Johann Gewirtz.' I showed the other side and read on. 'The Gobbling Galician.' (*see Oyster 4*).

'I know him! I know him!' Lady M — exclaimed. She took the dildo in her hand. A frown of concentration appeared on her forehead and she closed her eyes as though trying to recall some memory. 'It's just how I remember it.' She hefted it in her hand. 'Just like the original.'

'I'm sure I've never met a gentleman with his name inscribed on his prick, although I've seen some strange tattoos in Portsmouth,' said Megan.

'I don't mean the writing!' Lady M — said. 'But everything else is to the life.' She fondled it and pressed it to her. 'Would you mind, Gwendolen, if I were to use it? See,' she ran her finger down one side, 'where the lettering is raised up. That could stimulate fond recollections indeed.'

'I would be delighted if it would help you bring back the past,' said Gwendolen.

'I have every hope that it will also be a foretaste of things to come,' said Lady M —, 'for I have every expectation that he will be in these parts again shortly. He travels frequently.'

'There is one small problem,' said Cecily. 'If you are to enjoy Count Gewirtz and Gwendolen can make use of Andrew's facsimile, what am I to do? I am not sure that the original is yet in full working order.' Here she glanced at me.

Megan, who had been completely ignored during this division of the spoils, spoke up.

'There is my game,' she said. 'A game of chance with the winner taking first pick. Or prick?'

'A pottery lottery,' I said, rather pleased with my witticism.

'What an awful joke,' said Cecily. 'You will certainly have to pay a forfeit for that.'

'What *is* the game?' said Gwendolen. 'I can hardly wait to win. I am always lucky at cards.'

'Yes, we must get on with it,' said Lady M —. 'We have no idea when Mr Holmes may walk in and it would be nice to have a round or two completed before that happens.'

'It is simplicity itself,' said Megan. 'After I have shuffled the pack, we all take a card. The one with the lowest card has to take off some item of clothing. Then we repeat the procedure.'

'This could go on for hours,' said Lady M —.

'Not if we are quick about it,' said Cecily. 'Deal the cards!'

'Two!' said Cecily, peering under her card without turning it over. 'I lose.' With that she unbuttoned her dress and let it fall to the ground. Under her chemise, her splendid titties were delightfully outlined. Mr Pego responded happily.

'Cheat,' said Gwendolen. 'Turn it over. That's the rule. We must all see.'

'Oh Gwendolen, do you not trust me?' said Cecily. 'Surely old schoolfriends should have faith in one another. Do you not remember the School Motto?'

'No,' said Gwendolen. 'Anyway, it was in Latin and I

abhorred the language.' She turned Cecily's card over. 'Ten!' she said. 'I knew you were cheating. You must put your dress back on again this instant.'

'I don't think I can,' said Cecily. 'There are so many complicated buttons and things. You know I have never been very good at dressing myself.'

'Well, *I* have a five,' said Lady M — . 'I am certain that is a winning score.' She removed a glove.

I looked at her with admiration. I should explain that she had been a winner in previous rounds but had chosen to undress in an unorthodox order. Apart from her remaining glove she was completely naked. As the firelight played on her naked body, I began to have every confidence of being able to enter the game in the near future.

Again Megan dealt the cards. Again Cecily peeked at her card without letting the rest of us see. 'The Joker!' she said, a mischievous smile flitting across her face. 'That means I can take off ten items of clothing.'

'I don't remember that rule,' I said.

'Ask Megan,' said Cecily. 'You cannot have been paying proper attention when the rules were set out. I distinctly recall Megan saying so.'

Megan, sensing no doubt a certain mood of impatience among the assembled company, agreed to Cecily's statement with great promptness. 'I think that you were too tired to listen carefully at the beginning.'

'Very well,' I said. 'Ten items of clothing it shall be.'

Cecily, barely waiting for my concurrence, had slipped out of her chemise as well as her remaining underclothes.

'Seven choices left,' she said. 'But I have nothing left to remove. I believe that I have the right to allot my spare turns to anyone I may choose.' She looked round the room to see if there was any further disagreement.

'Dear Cecily,' said Gwendolen, 'I do hope that I can be the recipient of your generosity. I have been so unlucky in this game. I've hardly lost a stitch and I am beginning to find the heat from the fire quite enervating. I am sure I shall fall into a swoon unless I am able to get rid of some of these clothes.'

'But what about Megan,' I said. 'She also is unfortunately fully dressed. I think the two of you should share Cecily's gift.'

'Don't worry about me,' said Megan. 'Remember that if we all end up unclothed at the same time, the whole point of the game is lost.'

'You're right,' said Lady M — . 'Cecily and I are already out of the game, with nothing left to lose.'

With that, she picked up the two dildoes that had been left to warm in front of the grate.

'Cecily, if you would like to take Andrew, I have an urgent need to refresh my memory of dear Johnny.'

She flung herself down on the *chaise longue* and I watched with some envy as the Gewirtz dildo was thrust between her legs. Without any further ado, she began to slide it repeatedly in and out of her obviously eager quim. A satisfied look spread across her face.

'It's all coming back to me,' she said. 'Johnny Gewirtz to the life! It was at the Duchess of Hallamshire's Ball last winter. My husband was talking to some thoroughly boring people. I managed to evade his notice for a few minutes and Johnny Gewirtz and I escaped into a side room. I was simply dying for a fuck and he responded with all the gallantry for which foreign gentlemen are renowned. Although the fact that he was in the full dress uniform of some regiment or other delayed things for a while. The Gallician Cuirassiers! That was it. A very fanciful creation. A lot of gold and a positive chestful of medals, as well as a sword and spurs on his boots. There was no time to get that lot off so I pulled his trousers down and his military accoutrement fairly leaped out before me.'

As she reminisced, she was plying the object of her recollections rhythmically to and fro. Meanwhile Cecily, who had accepted her lot without complaint, was licking my likeness while making herself ready with her other hand. Then she knelt down on the hearth rug, facing the fire so that her splendid bum was staring us in the face. I realised from her movements that she was rubbing the dildo against her succulent breasts. Her back being turned to us as it was, I

170

could only guess what happened next. She gave an excited cry of pleasure and twitched her bottom. I realised that my likeness had been inserted into her delicious cunney.

So delightful was the scene that I at once knew that I should be able to take part in the activities without further delay.

'Would anyone like to sample the original?' I asked, taking hold of my prick and offering it to the room.

'Mine!' said Gwendolen, struggling frantically to get out of her clothes.

'Me!' said Cecily, looking round.

'Don't be selfish,' Gwendolen replied. 'You've got your plaything already.'

'Well, you're not ready,' said Cecily. 'Andrew, come over here!'

Rather ungallantly, I must admit, I abandoned poor Gwendolen to her disrobing and lined myself up behind Cecily. As soon as I grasped her by the hips, she lifted herself up and I entered into her from behind. She sighed and settled. Then she pulled forward again and removed herself from my impaling instrument.

'Both,' she said. 'I want to try both the copy and the original. They will have to take turns.' As Mr Pego stayed lodged between her thighs, she inserted my counterfeit into her and thrust it backwards and forwards several times. Then she pulled it out.

'Now the other,' she said. I slipped into her once more and drove on. Again she pulled clear and again I was replaced by my replica.

'All change again,' she cried out.

I realised that it was all a matter of timing. Three or four strokes were completed and then there was an exchange of instruments. Unusual though the situation was, it was nonetheless an exciting new sport. 'Always seek to broaden your experience,' I recalled young Fanny saying to me back in what now seemed my far distant school days. She had been parting the cheeks of her bum as she spoke, opening out her back passage into which she was urging me to enter. 'Tools rush in where angels fear to tread.' That had been another of her sayings. I had embraced her philosophy with gratitude.

Meanwhile Cecily had been speeding up her alternating members. As she became more rapid in her comings and goings, some confusions as to timing were beginning to creep in. More than once I found myself driving into her just as my other half was being withdrawn. She herself was now so widened that there was no question of her lips closing as one member slipped out. What with the heat from the fire and the heat of her exertions, she had become quite slippery with perspiration and her cunney juices were soaking into her bush and running down her thighs. I took my place once more.

'Stay in, Andrew!' she said, letting my replica fall from her hand. 'I want to be finished off by the real Thing.'

I took full responsibility and thrust on. Out of the corner of my eye, I spotted the approach of Gwendolen. Still partly dressed, she swooped on the discarded member and carried it off in triumph. Suddenly Cecily began to come.

While I tried to hold myself steady, she shuddered and started to moan, forcing herself onto me while her hands opened and closed, clawing at the rug, her whole body trembling with ecstasy. Like a stout anchor in a gale, I kept us safe and sound as the full storm of her coming burst upon us. Spasm after spasm coursed through her as she choked and gasped. Then she paused and gave out one last cry of delight before subsiding, still clamped about me, to the floor.

As I struggled to remain in her, I took the chance to survey the scene. Lady M— seemed quite transported by her memories of Johnny Gewirtz and was stretched out full length on her couch, one leg hooked up over the back and the other trailing on the ground, her hands grasping the object of her desire and forcing it slowly but regularly in and out of her tunnel of love.

Gwendolen was sitting on the floor, backed up against a comfortably upholstered chair. She had not bothered to complete her unrobing and her dress was pushed up to her waist. My discarded replica was being put to good use.

Megan, who was also fully dressed, was playing no part in the activities except that one hand had disappeared under her skirt. She was playing with herself as she stood by the window looking out into the street. All of a sudden she turned back into the room.

'Someone is coming,' she said.

'Almost everyone is coming,' I said.

'No! I mean outside!' she said urgently. 'There's a cab at the door and someone is getting out of it. It's Mr Holmes!'

Interesting though this news was, there was no-one other than myself sufficiently *compos mentis* to pay the least attention to it.

Withdrawing from Cecily's embrace, I joined Megan at the window, my prick still standing out like a tea-clipper's bowsprit.

'You could hang washing on that,' said Megan, taking hold of it and inspecting it with professionally dispassionate skill. 'But keep it away from the window panes, you're making them mist up with the heat.'

In spite of the rather domestic nature of her metaphor, I took it as a compliment. 'If you can make use of it,' I said, 'please do so.'

'As a working girl, I usually charge for such things,' she said. 'But I believe I may owe you some change from our first encounter. Anyway, there isn't the time now. Your Master is here.'

Sure enough, at that moment the door was opened and Holmes strode in.

'I see that you have been entertaining our guests,' he said, looking about him. Instinctively I dropped my hands, trying to conceal my straining member. Megan stood beside me, keeping her composure admirably in the circumstances. Neither Cecily, Gwendolen nor Lady M — reacted in any way whatsoever, so intent were they all on their activities.

'I, — I can explain — ' I said nervously.

'There is no need for explanations, Scott,' he said. 'It does not take a detective's training to understand what is going on. Pray, continue, Ladies,' he said to the others. 'But it would be nice if there was somewhere to sit.'

I pulled the only spare easy chair in the room over to him, but instead he remained standing. Then he began his familiar pacing to and fro.

'The plot is developing fast,' he said. 'I have uncovered the blackmailing swine who is behind it all.'

'Possibly we should attempt to engage Lady M — 's attention,' I said.

'She does not look like a woman who is capable of coherent thought at the moment,' he said, casting an eye on the display revealed to all and sundry on the *chaise longue*. 'My experience in these matters tells me that we will have to wait a little while longer.'

Lady M — was indeed oblivious to everything but her own imminent coming. She was spreadeagled, her head thrown back and clutching at Count Gewirtz' memento as though it was the last hold on life of a drowning sailor. Her magnificent breasts were rising and falling as she busied herself with her fast approaching climax.

As for the others, Cecily appeared to have fallen into a light sleep curled up in front of the fire, her hands between her thighs. Gwendolen, not yet so far gone along the path of pleasure, was backed up against her chair, her knees raised, making repeated insertions of my likeness. There was a frown of concentration on her face as she looked down on her deft probing and teasing. It was clear that she was concentrating all her efforts on her clit, rather than seeking the deepest penetration.

'Ring for Mrs Sayers, will you,' said Holmes to Megan. 'We are all about to need some restorative draft. Some Canary would be the most appropriate.' Then he looked at the mantelshelf. A small lacquered box that I had not seen before stood there. 'Fresh supplies from the Orient,' he said, picking it up. 'Lloyds confirmed that the ship was safely arrived in the Pool.'

The reference meant nothing to me but Holmes was obviously pleased. He prised open the tight-fitting lid of the box and sniffed delicately at the contents before reaching for his pipe. There followed the now familiar ritual of stuffing and tamping the smoking mixture into its capacious bowl. Finally he lit his pipe and sucked appreciatively at the stem.

'Not a habit of yours?' he asked me.

'I am a cigar man rather than a pipe smoker,' I answered.

174

'I have never been able to understand the enjoyment that there is to be got from such things.'

'There are pleasures in life that you have yet to sample, Scott,' he said. 'But you will come to them in your own good time.'

Megan meanwhile had been twitching her nostrils as the aromatic smoke rose. 'From the Levant,' she said.

'Ah, my dear, so you have a connoisseur's nose for such things,' said Holmes.

'I came across it when I was working in Portsmouth,' she said. 'When the Fleet was in. Particularly when any ship had returned from station in the Mediterranean.'

They exchanged little grins of complicity while I was left with the uneasy feeling that I was missing the point of their exchanges.

'But what of the plot?' I asked.

Holmes took his pipe out of his mouth and looked me up and down. I was suddenly conscious of the fact that I was stark naked and that Mr Pego was waving about as I talked. Holmes continued to look thoughtfully at me, one eyebrow raised as was his wont.

'Where is that charming dress you were wearing when I saw you last?' he said.

'Over there,' said Megan before I could gather my wits. 'On the floor in the corner. He threw it there when we started to play cards.'

'My dear,' he said to Megan, 'Could you do something about that?' He pointed to my plainly displayed pikestaff. 'I find it something of a distraction when I am trying to think.'

'Certainly, Sir,' she said.

Taking me carefully between finger and thumb she drew me aside. She began to squeeze my balls delicately but insistently. Then she knelt down in front of me. 'Soon have him discharged,' she said, looking up at Holmes. Then she took me in her mouth and, still massaging my balls, began to suck my straining cock. After my encounter with Cecily I was already close to my coming. Megan's skilled attentions soon provoked a first tingling response from my recharged testicles and then in no time at all I was beginning to feel a first surge of cum jetting down my prick. Megan held me in place and swallowed everything I could produce with consummate ease. After such an arduous day's duty, I was soon at the end although my pleasure remained unimpaired.

'That was quick,' said Holmes a moment or two later.

'He's had a busy time,' said Megan, practically wiping her lips delicately as the last drops leaked from my cock.

'And yours is a practised hand,' said Holmes.

'I am practised in all parts,' said Megan brightly. 'See, he's retreating out of sight already.'

'I suppose I owe you something for that?' I said to Megan, slightly put out by the way that I was being handled.

'No, no, allow me!' said Holmes, reaching into his pocket. 'I commissioned the job.'

'Sixpence, Sir,' said Megan.

'Your prices seem to be going up,' said Holmes.

'Special rates for the Gentry,' said Megan. 'I want to better myself in life.'

'Very sensible,' said Holmes. 'Always charge what the market will bear. One of the first lessons to be learned in commercial circles. However, now that Mr Scott is no longer intruding on my thought processes quite so visibly, I should perhaps begin to explain what I have been about since I left Lady M — 's.'

'And I shall account for myself also,' I said, anxious to demonstrate that I had not been delinquent in my duties as his assistant.

'I have a pretty shrewd idea of what has been happening as far as you and your friends are concerned,' said Holmes.

As he said this there was a positive howl of pleasure from the corner of the room. Gwendolen had achieved her aim of the moment. With a flamboyant gesture she fairly threw down my replica and began to laugh in sheer relief.

'I am sorry,' she said. 'But I did so need that. I do apologise for having interrupted your conversation. Pray continue. I will be quiet now.' She lay stretched out on the carpet like a cat in front of a fire, quite unconcerned that her bush was thus casually displayed.

'As I was saying,' said Holmes, 'much has taken place. I followed Lady M – 's visitor. He had his cab drop him off on the edge of Kensington Gardens. A man was waiting for him under a tree. A horse chestnut. *Aesculus Hippocastanum*, as it is known to the botanist.'

'Yes,' I said, somewhat impatiently.

'A man was waiting for him,' Holmes continued. 'They at once fell into urgent conversation. So intent were they that I was able to creep up on them unobserved.'

'So you were able to overhear what was said,' I interjected.

'Not a word,' said Holmes. 'Far too much wind. A south easterly.'

'How unfortunate,' I said.

'Not at all,' said Holmes. 'I was able to ascertain that money changed hands and that orders were being given. When, shortly afterwards, they parted, I followed the second man as he set off across the park. I had already made a tentative identification but my suspicions were soon confirmed. He crossed Bayswater Road and went into a house near Lancaster Gate. As he was admitted, he was clearly illuminated.'

'Who was it?' I asked eagerly.

'None other than Lord M – himself,' said Holmes. 'My earlier surmise was proved correct.' At this point there was a gasp. Lady M – had caught the sound of the name. She sat bolt upright, her breasts swaying most fetchingly as she clasped her knees together and looked up on us.

'My husband!' she said.

'Indeed yes,' said Holmes. 'You have been the victim of a dastardly scheme.'

'But what am I to do?' she said. 'He must have returned incognito from the Continent in order to spy on me. What a vile thing to do.'

'Do not upset yourself,' said Holmes. 'Now that we have found out all about his nasty little scheme, we can confront him with our knowledge and threaten to expose him to the Authorities.'

'But if this should become *public* knowledge, I shall never again be able to hold my head up in Society. I shall not be received anywhere and will have to retire to the country. I simply can't abide our place down in Wiltshire. It is huge and draughty and there is hardly anyone there one can fuck.'

'I do not think it will have to come to that,' said Holmes. 'I had in mind not some legal proceedings but a quiet word in the ear of one or two men of affairs close to the Prime Minister. That would be enough to ensure that he is never again employed on any missions of a diplomatic nature and that the Honour he so eagerly covets is never bestowed. There would be no public disgrace but word would get around and he would have to resign from his clubs. His days of influence would be at an end. Blackmail is frowned on in such circles. It casts doubt on one's suitability for much government work.'

'Nor can I bear the thought of having to confront him myself,' said Lady M —. 'In fact I never want to see the brute again. If he insists on taking up residence again in our house, I will have to leave at once and seek admission to some nunnery where he cannot find me.'

'I hardly think such drastic measures will be called for,' said Holmes. 'I will undertake to handle the whole distasteful business myself. I hope he does not become violent or I may be forced to knock the blackguard down.'

'His is a choleric disposition,' said Lady M —, 'and he is handy with his fists. He once brutally assaulted our Vicar in Wiltshire.'

'An unprovoked attack?' asked Holmes.

'Almost entirely so,' said Lady M —. 'I had had occasion to seek some spiritual comfort and advice and the Vicar had come to the house for that purpose. We were discussing my problems which involved, among others, a nice point of Trinitarian doctrine, when my husband burst into the bedroom quite unannounced and beside himself with rage. He accused the Vicar of intentions of a substantially secular nature and attacked him. The poor man was only able to save himself from further punishment by leaping from the window.

'Luckily there is a well-grown Virginia Creeper on that side of the house — '

178

'*Parthenocissus quinquefolia* or *tricuspidata*?' interrupted Holmes with his customary insistence on scientific accuracy.

'And he was able to scramble down to safety,' went on Lady M—, ignoring the interjection with aristocratic nonchalance. 'My husband flung his cassock, trousers and camera after him but he was in too much of a hurry to stop and pick them up. The curate was sent round for them the next day.

'After that, of course, I was no longer able to attend his services. Luckily the Living is in the gift of a neighbour with whom I have a close understanding, otherwise I am certain that the poor creature would have been turned out of pulpit and vicarage.'

'He sounds the sort of cleric a parish can ill afford to lose,' said Holmes. 'An incumbent with an understanding of the Sins of the Flesh from first hand experience is an asset to his flock.'

'He didn't have a very big Thing,' went on Lady M—, 'but he used it with a surprising degree of invention and precision, unlike my husband who is hung like a prize bull but who wields his weapon more like some medieval seige piece than an instrument of pleasure.

'The vicar also had the sweetest set of balls you have ever seen. When he became agitated, which was often in my presence, they used to swing from side to side like an incense censer being processed down the aisle in a Roman church.'

'A charming picture,' said Holmes, 'but we must complete our plans. Have you any idea who may own the Lancaster Gate house where he appears to be staying?'

'In all probability his cousin Humphrey, a morbid sort of fellow; tall, cadaverous and unsmiling with a stern moral view of Humanity. I only once saw him show any signs of animation and that was when I was telling him of my work with Fallen Women. He expressed deep interest in the Home I was establishing for them and enquired after the means of Correction that were to be used on the inmates.

'I recall that he gave me something of a lecture on the virtues of physical chastisement in cases of moral backsliding. He seemed to regard his own hand as an extension of the

179

Divine Will. He belongs to a like-minded group who call themselves Spankers for the Lord. They devote much of their spare time to what they call Visitations. As many as a dozen of them will descend on a place, usually one of the poorer parts of some Northern manufacturing town, and seek out women of the streets and back alleys. They urge them into the Paths of Repentance, exhorting them to bend before the storms of Righteousness and belabouring their buttocks to drive out Sinfulness. I am told that the sounds of their Redemptive Onslaughts fairly ring through the meaner streets of the North. They have a particular liking for Oldham. At the end of their expeditions, they repair to Buxton or Matlock, sore-handed and worn out with their efforts, and take the waters.'

'I had a Gentleman in Wales who was similarly inclined,' said Megan. 'An Elder of one of the stricter Chapels in Aberavon I think it was. He used to seek me out every Thursday. I had to lean over a table while he smacked my bum and cried out to the Heavens that here was a miserable sinner who had to be driven firmly along the road to Rectitude. I charged him sixpence. I used to point out that he could have a fuck for tuppence but he didn't seem to be interested in that sort of thing.

'He used to sing a sort of hymn while he was chastising me. "Spanking out the Sin" it was called. He used to beat out the time on my bottom. Of course, we Welsh are a musical nation.'

At this point I recalled the apoplectic man in the upturned dogcart whom we had encountered while bicycling in Northamptonshire (*see Oyster 4*). However Holmes, who had been listening to these digressions with avid interest, decided now to recall us to our present planning before I could recount my own tale of Fundamental Practices.

'Is Cousin Humphrey likely to be a party to your husband's blackmail plot?' he asked Lady M — . 'Is he for instance likely to be in need of additional funds in order to finance his spanking expeditions?'

'I doubt it very much,' said Lady M — . 'He has a substantial private income. He is in any case by profession an attorney and I have never found such people to be short of funds.'

'In that case,' said Holmes, 'I will call at the house in the morning. I think you had better accompany me, Scott. The presence of two able-bodied visitors will dissuade our quarry from attempting any violence when we confront him with our suspicions.'

'What if he is not at home?' I asked.

'We will wait for him,' said Holmes. 'We can explain that we have an urgent communication of a confidential nature from the Foreign Office. We must take the photographs with us and ensure that we do not come away without the original plates.'

'But what shall *I* do?' said Lady M—. 'I do not want to return home until I am assured that my husband is not likely to call.'

'You must stay here,' said Holmes. 'Mrs Sayers will see that you have every comfort.'

'And we can safely go home,' said Cecily, 'unless, dear Priscilla, you would feel more at ease if we stayed here with you.'

'Thank you, I should like that,' said Lady M—.

'In that case,' said Holmes, 'Megan might like to stay as well. She is already so involved in the case that I am sure she would like to know of the outcome. I would also like to discuss the possibility of the payment of a retainer fee. An occasional additional pair of eyes and ears is always of use to someone in my line of business.'

'Thank you, Sir,' said Megan. 'Would you like a fuck on account?'

'Not now,' said Holmes hastily. 'I need to consider tomorrow's encounter. Possibly Mr Scott would like to act on my behalf.'

'I doubt if he has got it in him,' said Gwendolen sweetly.

'Please do not make such assumptions,' I said stiffly.

'Now we've upset him,' said Cecily. 'Andrew,' she continued, 'I for one do not want to cast aspersions on your prowess. Possibly a good hot bath would restore you to your customary vigour.'

181

'That is easily arranged,' said Holmes, 'but I shall have to leave it to you to attend to his recuperation. I am certain he will be in good hands.'

Lady M — looked up. 'What an excellent idea,' she said. 'I would like to see him revived and besides, the endeavour would help me take my mind off this whole sorry business.'

Soon afterwards I found myself happily immersed in a hot bath. Megan was holding Mr Pego up out of the water as she soaped and sponged my sorely tried balls, while Gwendolen and Cecily knelt beside the bath, scrutinising her efforts.

'I do not think there is any more need to hold him up,' said Cecily. 'He seems to be recovering.' Megan released me and sure enough, Mr Pego managed to stay upright. She stepped back in order to inspect me.

'We'd better give him a complete scrubbing,' said Cecily. 'Gwendolen and I will start with his feet.'

In no time at all, three pairs of hands were employed about my person.

'Close your eyes,' said Cecily, 'We've got to get you clean from head to toe.'

I did as I was told and surrendered myself to their solicitous attentions. Gentle hands soaped and lathered my body. Fatigue and pleasure coursed through me and lulled me into a half-conscious daze. My eyes closed and I drifted while the pains and strains of the day were drained from my over-taxed body.

Suddenly I jumped convulsively as though an electric shock has been passed through me. A sharp fingernail had been run up the tender underside of my prick.

'Keep your eyes shut or you will get soap in them,' said a stern voice.

Lady M — had decided to take charge. There came a sound of giggling and my legs were lifted up and parted so that my ankles rested on the rim on either side of the bath. An unseen hand began gently to massage my balls. Then first one and then the other big toe was encircled by a warm mouth. I flinched.

'He's ticklish!' came a gleeful voice. 'What fun!'

Two tongues licked and rasped at the soles of my feet. I struggled convulsively to get free but as I thrashed about, my head went under the water just as I tried to draw in a deep breath. As my lungs filled, I spluttered, spouted and flailed wildly about. Water cascaded everywhere and there were peals of laughter. I sat bolt upright, blinking vigorously to get the water out of my eyes.

'Now look what you've done,' said Lady M — . 'His Thing has sunk down out of sight. Just lie back again Andrew and think of England. We have no intention of drowning you.'

Pinioned as I was, I had no real option but to obey. As I lowered myself backwards, Mr Pego floated back up from the depths to lie on the surface and then slowly begin his resurrection.

'That's better,' said Megan.

'I can think of a part for me in all this,' said Lady M — . Unbuttoning herself, she leaned over me. Two dark nipples swayed like forbidden fruit just above my face. Tantalisingly they were lowered to within an inch of my mouth. I strained up towards them, poking out my tongue to touch them but they trembled teasingly just out of reach.

'Like a stranded fish, he is,' said Megan. 'Don't be so cruel, Ma'am.'

Lady M — cupped her breasts in her hands, pushing them out towards me and letting them brush my face. Then like a suckling infant, I managed to latch on to a nipple and began to suck hungrily at it. Lady M — pulled away slightly and, for a distressing moment, I thought I was to be deprived of my comfort. Craning my head upwards I tried to retain my hold. Then she relented and lowered herself once more. Greedily I pulled at her swollen nipple, aware at the same time that Mr Pego was standing proudly above the water like a palm tree on a desert island, except in his case the nuts were at the bottom rather than hanging from the top.

With Lady M — 's splendid bosom now pressed against my face and my vision thus delightfully obscured, I was unable to see whose was the mouth that now descended on my upright member, taking in half of his length in one gulp. At the same time I became aware that other soft breasts were stroking my feet, one to either side of the bath. More water was displaced as I stretched out, rubbing against them while at the same time forcing Mr Pego up and further into the friendly mouth.

'The floor is absolutely soaking,' came a voice. 'Shouldn't we get him out of there before the whole place is turned into a swamp.'

'It's far too late to worry about a thing like that,' came an answer. 'As long as we all help to clear up afterwards, I expect we will be able to make our peace with Mr Holmes and the housekeeper. Besides, I've just had an idea!'

As I nuzzled at Lady M – 's plump and responsive titties, moving from one to the other and feeling first one nipple and then the other harden in my mouth, I was aware of whispering. All at once there was an almighty splash and a veritable tidal wave shot along the bath. Still clinging on to Lady M – 's bountiful breast, I nearly disappeared under water once again as a soapy torrent filled my eyes and nostrils. I spluttered and lost my grip but as the waters washed over me and I went down for the second time, I was dimly aware that I was no longer alone in the bath.

A naked woman was kneeling between my legs while Megan held out my cock to her like the priest of some strange religion holding out a votive offering. Before I could ascertain whether it was Cecily or Gwendolen who had joined me in my ablutions, I was once more submerged. Peering up through the water, I saw the distorted outlines of Lady M – 's wonderful breasts looming above me. As the tide swirled over me and then began to recede, I bobbed to the surface again, only to collide with her generous flesh. This had the unfortunate effect of pushing me under once more just as I reached up with my mouth to the life-saving nipple that swam before me.

With a gurgle I sank to the bottom but, as all my past life began to pass before me, someone grabbed me by the hair and I was jerked upwards.

'Quick, pull out the plug,' came Megan's voice. Spluttering and spitting out water, I took in a much-needed lungful of air. In my struggles I had thoroughly drenched Lady M —. Trickles of water ran down her succulent breasts and dripped from her nipples into my open mouth. I swallowed once and then again, licking the droplets as they hung, ready to fall.

Then, as the receding water flowed past me, my newly-arrived companion slid towards me along the fast-emptying bath and with the truest of aims, impaled herself on my prick. Easing herself backwards and forwards, she began to fuck me. Lady M — 's hands were cradling the back of my head, pulling me on to her and keeping me away from any abrupt and painful contact with the taps. Realising that I was not about to die and that I was in safe hands, I began to respond, pushing forward to help my member in its repeated entries into that warm, receptive cunney.

'He's better,' came a voice. 'For an awful moment I thought he'd overtaxed his strength.'

'At least his most vital part is back in the land of the living,' said another. 'Just look at it!'

'Thank Heavens,' said the first voice. 'I'm certain Mr Holmes would never have forgiven us if he'd lost his new assistant so suddenly.'

'He would indeed have been a great loss to the world,' said another. 'Although, of course, there would always have been the Scott dildo to remember him by.'

'I for one would have insisted that it was placed in perpetuity on his gravestone. At least it wouldn't have wilted like a bunch of flowers and future generations would have been able to appreciate what had distinguished him in life.'

'People would have come from miles around to stroke it for luck and in fond remembrance. It would have become all worn and shiny like the toe on that saint's statue in Rome that the pilgrims always kiss.'

'Or the Blarney stone.'

'Except that as it became all weathered and worn down, no one would think it was anything out of the ordinary any more and they'd stop coming.'

'And the moss would grow over it.'

'Sad.'

Sic transit gloria pudendi.

I tried to interrupt this increasingly heartless conversation but Lady M – 's bountiful bosom once more stopped up my mouth. Meanwhile I was slipping and squeaking my way up and down the nearly empty bath in my efforts to keep pace with the eager quim that had swallowed up my revived member and was now bumping and boring against me.

'Ow!' said a Welsh voice as someone fell over with a thump. 'The whole floor is sopping wet and slippery. Help me up someone, please!'

'Your dress is wringing wet,' came what I dimly realised was Gwendolen's voice. 'Here let me help you off with it. It will have to be hung up somewhere to dry.'

By now I was growing increasingly uncaring of what exactly was going on around me as the excitement of my fuck in the bath grew with every stroke. I drove on, thrust following thrust until, locked together, we began to skid wildly along the bath.

'He's got the soap wedged under his bum,' said Megan, spotting that something was awry. 'He's going to do himself an injury if we don't get it out.'

I was grasped under the cheeks of my bum and hoisted up while another hand insinuated itself under me, groping around until it closed on the unwanted bar of soap.

'Bother,' came Megan's voice, 'it's got away again. I can't see where it's gone. We'll have to try and anchor him in position until Miss Cardew has finished.'

I was steadied and held in position as Cecily moved more and more vigorously up and down my prick. She was beginning to breathe heavily. With Gwendolen and Megan holding on to my feet and Lady M – supporting my head, I was able to hold steady as her movements rose to a frenzy.

'The insatiable in pursuit of the immovable,' observed Gwendolen as she gritted her teeth, clinging on to me for dear life.

'I'm coming! I'm coming!' Cecily cried out.

My knuckles were white with the effort of holding on to the sides of the bath. I tensed myself as her cunney almost swallowed me up. She let out a great shriek of pleasure and I felt her shudder all over as her juices flowed down. I was so deep in her that it felt as though I should never be able to retrace her passage. I could feel the sorely tried end of my prick probing her innermost being while she seized me by the hips and tried to force me even further into her. Desperately I thrust back, aware that the mixture of cum and soap had made the bath so treacherous that any slip could result in serious injury. She shrieked again and gave one last heave before almost collapsing. A couple of great sighs wracked her body and she lay back, her breasts rising and falling with the effort that she had put into her fucking.

We lay still for a moment and then, as the others relaxed their grip on me, inch by inch my swollen, glistening member slipped out of her. Lady M — 's generous bosom ceased to press against me. I licked feebly at a passing nipple and then, utterly exhausted, lay still, my undischarged firing piece pointing at the ceiling.

'He can't go to sleep there,' said Gwendolen firmly, after a blissful moment or two of rest. 'Andrew! Pull yourself together and get up!'

Wearily, I struggled upright. Willing arms supported me as I stepped out on to the wet floor. With the whole bath now to herself, Cecily stretched out full length. I looked down at her. Drops of water hung like fresh dew on the hairs of her pussey, trembling slightly as she breathed. Her wonderful big titties stood proud above her ribcage. Her eyes were open but with a faraway look in them, while a big silly grin spread over her face.

Pride stirred in me at the thought that even in my exhausted state, I had been able to satisfy her once more. I lifted my chin and squared my shoulders.

'It's all right,' I said, shrugging off my supporters. 'I can stand up.' Megan, Gwendolen and Lady M — let go of me and I collapsed.

That night, or rather during the remainder of the night, I slept the sleep of the dead. Who put me to bed I do not know, nor who brought the bowl of sustaining broth. Truly I had been driven to the limits of human endurance. Like some explorer

187

in the Dark Continent struggling through the jungles, or the master of a ship, thrusting its way through the ice floes of the Greenland Sea in search of the North West Passage, I had endured and survived. As I closed my eyes, visions of pussies swam before me. I reached down to touch my trusty tool. It was also dead to the world. All I could hope was that we would both wake in the morning. I snuggled down and lapsed into unconsciousness.

'Mrs Sayers reports that you acquitted yourself nobly last night,' said Holmes.

We were swaying along in a cab, *en route* to the Lancaster Gate house and our rendezvous with the unsuspecting Lord M — . I had been roused at what had seemed an unearthly hour. I was still deeply fatigued but determined not to let Holmes realise my weakened state.

'Although she was left with rather a lot of clearing up to do,' he went on. 'Wet clothing everywhere. She's getting rather rheumaticky in the knees and all that bending down and picking things up is not good for her. Luckily Megan helped. When I left they were doing the washing up together.'

'Washing up?' I said. 'I do not recall a meal.'

'Soup bowls and dildoes,' said Holmes. 'At least two of the latter, recently used. Obviously they belonged to our guests. If they have need of them again while we are out, they can be found on the draining board.'

I accepted the reprimand. It was true that his rooms had been left in some disarray, although I had not personally been responsible for much that had gone on and for the life of me I did not know what I could have done to persuade our guests to behave with more decorum. I decided to change the subject.

'The blackmailer's photographs,' I said. 'There appear to be two sets: one that was presented to Lady M — as evidence of her activities, and a second, sent to you by her husband with a request that you discover the identities of the intruding members. You suggested when Lady M — first arrived that the pictures had been taken by her husband. Surely he would have recognised the gentlemen involved. Or at least some of them?'

'The answer to your question, Scott, is that, whilst he took the photographs, he was not actually present at the time.'

'I don't understand,' I said.

'The explanation is quite simple,' said Holmes. 'Last night, I took the liberty of inspecting the marital bedroom at Lady M — 's. I found a thin but strong wire attached to one of the legs of the bed. It led through a small hole carefully bored in the wainscoting, into the next room, up the wall and back into a loft space immediately above the bedroom. A spyhole had been cut in the ceiling. It was almost invisible from below since there is some intricate plaster moulding that hides it. I peered through the hole. It is lined up precisely on the bed. In the loft were traces of powder burns and indentations in the dust.

'A camera must have been positioned there, lined up on the bed. Because of the restricted field of vision, only a few square inches of any visitor could be seen.'

'And the camera would be triggered off by any pronounced movement of the bed,' I said. 'Such as that occasioned by a bout of fucking.'

'Precisely,' said Holmes. 'Exposure below would be followed by exposure above. No doubt there were many times when the bodies were not lined up with the lens and nothing of interest was recorded, but so great and so frequent is that poor creature's need for consolation in her unhappy marriage, that some at least were likely to be recorded *in flagrante delicto* as the lawyers would say.'

'And you have in fact made some identifications of the instruments of pleasure involved?' I asked.

'I have narrowed down the field considerably,' said Holmes, 'to the point where I could make a positive identification with only a little more research if I so chose.' He drew out the portfolio and showed it to me.

'For instance, this fellow here,' he continued, picking one specimen out. 'What do you make of that?'

I scrutinised the proffered print. 'There seem to be indentations on it,' I said.

'Precisely,' Holmes said. 'Those are literally indentations. It has been recently bitten. Notice an irregularity in the markings. You will have discerned when Lady M— smiles, that she has a small gap between two of her front teeth. I am prepared to wager that she is the biter. In addition Dr Motson, if he were here, would doubtless be able to confirm that the extent of the injuries is such that the victim would have had to seek medical treatment after the event. There are only two doctors in London who specialise in such matters. I will not name names but one is By Appointment to the Prince of Wales while the other is a Harley Street man with a practice consisting largely of military patients. Either, if it was explained that this was a matter of National importance, would doubtless be prepared to tell me in the strictest confidence if they had treated such a wound recently. However, as I said, I do not intend to pursue the matter any further.'

'What of the others?' I asked.

'The one with the Masonic insignia tattooed on the forearm: that is the mark of a very secret lodge restricted to senior members of the Church of England. Among their number, the Bishop of Y— has a reputation in clerical circles for his zealousness in offering spiritual comfort to unhappy women, especially among the aristocracy.'

'And the remainder?'

'These two would appear to be identical twins. They could almost be the same member except that in one case, it has been recently exposed to the elements while the other is a very pale specimen. So we are looking for brothers, one of whom regularly engages in open air fucking. A countryman, in all probability a Scotsman, ever prepared to lift up his kilt as he goes about his country pursuits. His brother I suspect would prove to be a town dweller. Both were captured on the same occasion judging by the similar wrinkles in the small area of bed linen visible. So I suspect that we are looking at a Scotsman who is in Town, visiting his twin brother. An estate North of the Border and a business in London points to an interest in the whisky trade. The McShaftoe of that Ilk and his brother, known in his locality as the Bane of Speyside, are the most likely candidates.'

'Amazing!' I said. 'And have you made any more identifications?'

'One,' he said. 'Where have you seen something like this before?'

He held out a further print. I peered closely at it. There was indeed a familiarity about the object of our attentions. Suddenly I remembered.

'The other dildo!' I said. 'This is the original of the Gewirtz instrument. The one that was signed.'

'I took the liberty of inspecting it after it had been laid out to dry by the sink in the kitchen,' said Holmes. 'A remarkable piece of work.'

'What do you intend to do with the photographs, assuming that we are successful in our interview with Lord M — ?' I asked.

'Lady M — 's set, I will return to her. She may wish to destroy them or to keep them as souvenirs. That is up to her. The original plates will be destroyed and the second set of prints will be lodged in my forensic library. They may come in handy at some time in the future. A good reference library is invaluable to the detective.'

I recalled Rosie the Errant Schoolgirl (*see Oyster 3*).

'A friend of mine is in a position to lay her hands on a magnificent collection of photographic records of female bottoms,' I said. 'Many of them are those of the pupils at a well-thought-of school in the West Country. The owner is in the process of developing a system of identification and classification of types based on the human bum. It is his life's work and he has sacrificed much to continue his work.'

'I should like to hear his theory,' said Holmes. 'You must put me in touch with him. The scientific mind must be encouraged.'

Shortly afterwards, the cab slowed to a halt.

'Ah, we have arrived,' said Holmes. 'Now to beard the beast in his den.'

I do not intend to describe the painful interview that followed. Suffice it to say that we left a broken man in

Lancaster Gate. The threat of exposure was enough. The plates were handed over and we returned to Marylebone Road. Lady M – was so delighted at the successful outcome of our visit that she left me with a standing invitation to visit her and enjoy her hospitality as soon as I was sufficiently recovered to pay her the attentions she sought.

'We shall be At Home on Wednesday,' said Cecily as she and Gwendolen left. 'A Musical Afternoon. You might consider bringing a friend with you. It will be an energetic occasion.'

'A quick fuck?' offered Megan, before she too went on her way.

I had to decline her offer, being still somewhat drained by the events of the last few days. She was most understanding and announced that in any case, she would be a regular visitor to Holmes' establishment since it had been agreed that she would be assisting him as the occasion demanded.

It remains only to be said that a small paragraph in *The Times*, a day or so later, noted that Lord M – had sailed from Liverpool on a prolonged visit to one of our more obscure Colonies. He was not expected to return in the foreseeable future.

By then I was safely ensconced in Mrs P – 's Bayswater house where I had been given a rapturous welcome by her daughters. So ended my first exhausting venture into the world of Crime and Punishment.